BAD Mermaids

On Thin Ice

Books by Sibéal Pounder

BAD Mermaids
On Thin Ice

SIBÉAL POUNDER

Illustrated by
Jason Cockcroft

BLOOMSBURY
CHILDREN'S BOOKS
LONDON OXFORD NEW YORK NEW DELHI SYDNEY

BLOOMSBURY CHILDREN'S BOOKS
Bloomsbury Publishing Plc
50 Bedford Square, London WC1B 3DP, UK

BLOOMSBURY, BLOOMSBURY CHILDREN'S BOOKS and the Diana logo
are trademarks of Bloomsbury Publishing Plc

First published in Great Britain in 2019 by Bloomsbury Publishing Plc

A catalogue record for this book is available from the British Library

ISBN: PB: 978-1-4088-7716-6; eBook: 978-1-4088-7717-3

2   4   6   8   10   9   7   5   3   1

Typeset by RefineCatch Limited, Bungay, Suffolk
Printed and bound in Great Britain by CPI Group (UK) Ltd, Croydon CR0 4YY

MIX
Paper from
responsible sources
FSC® C020471

To find out more about our authors and books visit www.bloomsbury.com
and sign up for our newsletters

For my marvellous pal Nicola,
because of the seal bit

BELUGA
TOWN

SALMON CITY

North America

OCTOPOLLI

PINKLY LAGOON

THE HIDDEN LAGOON

Pacific Ocean

South America

Atlantic Ocean

The Mermaid World Map

Arctic Ocean

...AMBERBERG

Europe

Asia

HERMIT GROVE

THE KINGDOM OF MUME

...rica

JEWELPORT

FORTRESS BAY

RAINBOW LANDING

THE CROCODILE KINGDOM

Australia

Indian Ocean

FROSTOPIA

Antarctica

Last Time in Mermaid World...

The gang grew bigger! At first it was just Beattie and her twin best friends, Mimi and Zelda – and, of course, Steve, the talking seahorse. But now they have Paris too. She's a human who, with the help of a magic necklace, can morph into a mermaid and various other sea creatures. And in the Crocodile Kingdom, they befriended Gronnyupple, the Seahorse Surprise-guzzling water witch, who told Beattie she's a water witch too! And they also figured out Mimi is a fishtalker. So that's the gang – two water witches, one fishtalker, a human who can morph into a mermaid, a talking seahorse and a ... Zelda.

When we left them, they were on their way to Frostopia in a clam car. Gronnyupple is convinced Maritza Mist is in trouble. Maritza is also a water witch and she owns the *Maritza Mist's Water Witch Catalogue*, where

all water witches order their magic. Gronnyupple didn't receive her latest catalogue order, which made her suspect something had happened to Maritza – and when they heard that two immortal mermaids who had used Maritza's magic potions had escaped from Viperview Prison, they started to worry. So they set off to find her.

But getting into Frostopia is a challenge because the kingdom is closed to mermaids from other realms. Beattie is hoping they'll be able to glide in undetected, which is wishful thinking because nothing ever seems to go to plan...

First, though, it's time to check in on a mermaid called Meri, in the far-off – and much warmer – underwater city of Fortress Bay. Because that's where this story *really* begins...

1

Meri Pebble, the Spy Mermaid

Meri Pebble had been a Fortress Bay spy for as long as she could swish her tail, and her morning routine was *always* the same.

She swam out of bed, a fish brushed her teeth, and she pulled her long black hair into a slick ponytail. Then she ate some of her favourite Sandcrackle cereal.

After breakfast, Meri collected her jellyfish assistant, Lady Wriggles, and together they swam to the northerly tower of Fortress Bay headquarters to do their morning rounds.

Only on this particular morning, she was running very late.

'Excuse me, coming through,' Meri said as she wriggled her way past all the spy mermaids crowding

the corridors. Meri was Fortress Bay's most promising young spy, so she had some special extra duties that none of the other mermaids knew about.

As she swam along, she swished her tail from side to side, making images flash across it. Her spy-mermaid tail looked plain and ordinary, but she could see pictures from all around the world on it. Spy mermaids kept an eye on former criminal mermaids, human divers who needed distracting and whales assisting with spy missions. Meri loved watching the mermaids of the underwater kingdoms, all free and having fun. They had no idea what dangers she was protecting them from.

Sometimes she wished she could be like them, but she couldn't leave Fortress Bay until her training was complete. And spy training took *years*.

In a quiet corridor she pressed her tail against a metal panel. Lady Wriggles did the same, only with her little jellyfish face. The panel glowed and clicked back to reveal a room beyond – a room filled with frost and freezing water.

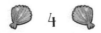

'Do you want to see who can create the biggest nose icicles today?' Meri asked Lady Wriggles.

Lady Wriggles rearranged her tentacles into a NO. She never wanted to play that game.

'Suit yourself,' Meri said with a smile as the door closed behind them. Frost formed on her jet-black hair as she swam deeper inside.

'Spy MP 241 reporting from Tower Five, secret lock four,' she said, slotting her tail into a gap in the floor.

There was another click and Meri rose out of the ground on a platform. In front of her, another piece of the floor rose too – a thick tube, dark and frozen.

Lady Wriggles began punching buttons on a control panel.

Meri gave her a nod. 'Spy MP 241 illuminating the ice narwhal.'

A light burst from the tube.

'Spy MP 241 speaking. I can confirm that the ice narwhal is—'

Her eyes grew wide.

'Gone!'

Lady Wriggles looked like she'd been electrified.

'And the list?' Meri said, her eyes darting to the back of the door, where a very important list was kept.

The list had vanished.

'Whoever took the ice narwhal also took the list,' Meri said. 'Oh this is bad. Quick, Lady Wriggles. *The telephone.*'

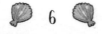

Meri paused.

'We can't mention this to anyone, Lady Wriggles. We'll be in so much trouble. We've got to get it back before anyone finds out.'

Lady Wriggles rearranged her tentacles into an Mmmmm.

'Please,' Meri begged.

'*Swim Together, Sink Together*' was the mermaid spy and sea-creature assistant pledge – Lady Wriggles had very little choice in the matter.

'Oh, and one more thing,' Meri went on. 'Please could you make a fake replacement ice narwhal? Just until I find the real one.'

Lady Wriggles reluctantly scooped up some ice from the floor and squished it into shape.

Meri placed it in the tube. 'Good narwhal sculpting! Now, the telephone.'

The jellyfish swam off and returned with a human phone.

A fish popped out of the receiver to take the message, because that's how mermaids make phone calls.

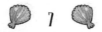

'CODE BLUE, CODE BLUE. Urgent message to be delivered to Maritza Mist of Realm Nine, Frostopia. The ice narwhal is GONE.'

2

Zelda on Thick Ice

Beneath the freezing waters of Antarctica, Frostopia's perfect ice walls rose from the depths. It was a mermaid kingdom that didn't let outsiders in. A familiar clam car floated nearby, but only Beattie was in it.

'*Oh I do like to be in Frostopiaaaaa! Oh I do like to be stuck to a waaaalllll!*' Zelda sang – from where she was frozen, upside down on the city's outer wall.

Zelda was impulsive. She liked taking risks, playing shockey – which she was excellent at – and annoying Steve, Beattie's talking seahorse.

'MY EARS ARE SCREAMING – you're *so* out of tune!' Steve said as Paris and Mimi tried to pull Zelda free.

'Only because I'm upside down,' Zelda shot back.

'Stop wriggling,' Mimi and Paris said at once, as they tried in vain to peel Zelda off the wall.

 9

Mimi, Zelda's twin, was acquainted with her antics. Paris, on the other hand, was still getting used to her.

'Why is Zelda's tail making such a squeaking noise?' Beattie whispered. 'We'll be heard for miles around!'

'Oh calm down,' Zelda said. 'Look, there's no one here.'

Beattie didn't know why she bothered trying to keep them all out of trouble. She was almost always unsuccessful.

'What if we slide her down the wall by yanking her hair?' Paris suggested.

Zelda scowled. 'No one touches my hair.'

'I know!' Gronnyupple said as she rifled around in her backpack and pulled out a tiny potion bottle.

She lobbed the bottle at Zelda. It exploded, spreading a strange green gloop everywhere. Zelda's perfectly flicked green hair began flashing.

'Hmm …' Gronnyupple said. 'That was meant to free you, but instead it's turned your hair … into a shining beacon.'

'Great,' Beattie groaned, hitting her head repeatedly off the clam-car steering wheel.

'Beattie ...' Gronnyupple said. 'I see Frostopia mermaids ...'

Zelda tried to turn. 'I can't see them! I can just see... bright-green light.'

Steve dived into his false teeth, making them snap shut.

Gronnyupple was right. In the distance, Beattie could make out two mermaids, their tails decorated with icicles and their hair an electric shade of blue. They rode on the backs of killer whales with SECURITY written in thick frost across their noses.

'Hurry!' Beattie hissed at the others, pointing madly at the mermaids.

'Uh-oh,' Mimi said.

Gronnyupple shook her head in disbelief. '*How* did they see us?'

Beattie stared at Zelda's flashing hair. 'I suppose it will always be a mystery.'

'I hope we don't get eaten,' Gronnyupple said quietly

as she shoved some Seahorse Surprise sweets in her mouth.

'Eaten?' Beattie gulped.

Gronnyupple shrugged and pointed at the whale on the left. 'I know a hungry face when I see one.'

Beattie gave the Frostopia mermaids a shy wave, but they glided straight past her and halted next to Zelda.

'It's not what you think,' Zelda said quickly. Her face had gone purple from being upside down for too long, and her hair was still flashing.

They floated in awkward silence until one of the mermaids steered his whale towards the clam car and leaned inside.

'I've never seen a clam car like this before,' he said.

The other mermaid swam down and peered in the passenger window. 'Aha!'

Beattie froze.

'I KNOW WHO YOU ARE,' the mermaid said.

Beattie's tail began to shake. The false teeth next to her started to chatter – which meant Steve was scared too.

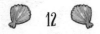

'You're Gillica and the team!' the mermaid said, flashing her a smile. 'We've been expecting you.'

'I'm not Gill—' Beattie began, but Zelda cut her off.

'That's right … I'm Gillica! Can Gillica get unstuck from the wall now, please?'

'Excellent,' the one on the left said, swivelling her whale around and shouting 'RELEASE!' Zelda slipped from the wall and dived into the clam car.

Steve tutted at her.

They watched as the security mermaids swam off and began rearranging icicles on the wall.

'Cool,' Paris said. 'It must be a secret pattern code to get in!'

'Zelda,' Beattie hissed. 'How are we supposed to get out of this one?'

'I think what you meant to say, Beattie, is thank you *so much*, Zelda, for saving us from being eaten by a security whale.'

The whale looked offended.

'He says that's a really offensive stereotype,' Mimi

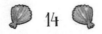

said. Mimi was a fishtalker and she could understand sea creatures.

'The sea must be so loud for you,' Paris said, but Mimi was concentrating on the whale.

'And anyway,' she continued, 'he had a big breakfast, so at most he'd only be eating two of us.'

The whale shifted its gaze to Steve.

'And probably Steve,' Mimi added.

'Eat me?' Steve scoffed. 'But I'm wearing *COUTURE*.'

Mimi stared at the whale for a second and nodded. 'The whale says he doesn't know what that is.'

'Get ready, great and honourable guests!' the security mermaid shouted, turning her whale to face the wall. 'Frostopia awaits!'

The icicles began to glow and the wall started to crack, revealing an icy tunnel that dipped down into the darkness below.

'WOAH,' everyone said at once (apart from Steve, who said 'CRIPES!' – which was a word he was trying to bring back).

'Line up your clam car and keep the engine turned

off, please,' the security mermaid said. 'Let the ice tunnel do the work ... AND MAY I BE THE FIRST TO SAY WE CANNOT *WAIT* FOR YOUR SHOW!'

'Show?' Paris whispered. 'What show?'

'And Gillica, who is me, cannot wait either,' Zelda said awkwardly, giving Beattie a wink.

Beattie gritted her teeth and reluctantly drove the clam car towards the mouth of the tunnel. As soon as the car made contact, the water got even colder and she began to shiver.

Steve pointed his tail at his fur cone top. 'Always dress for the occasion,' he said. 'And preferably in couture. You'll have to go shopping for a new outfit once we get to Frosto—'

The clam car dropped, hurtling faster and faster until they were pinned to the ceiling of the clam car.

'PPPPPPPP-IIIIIIIIIIIIIII-AAAAAAAAAA!' Steve finished.

Miraculously, they had found a way into a mermaid kingdom that had not been seen for years. A kingdom of myths, legends and magic!

 16

And hopefully a shop that sold warm stuff.

'ARE WE NEARLY THERE?' Paris shouted, her hair and eyelashes frosting over.

There was a little click and they slipped out of the tunnel. Icicles exploded around them like fireworks, and curtains of ice fish parted as their speed reduced. And that's when Beattie saw it – the icy realm of Frostopia, frozen beneath them. It was bigger than the Hidden Lagoon and the Crocodile Kingdom combined!

'Maritza Mist is down there somewhere,' Gronnyupple said as she peeled a bag of Seahorse Surprise off her face. 'And we're going to find her!'

It wasn't going to be easy, and Frostopia's magic meant the realm stretched further than anyone could see …

3

Blubble the Ice-skating Seal

Frostopia was unlike anything Beattie could have imagined. Huge frozen towers rose up from the depths, connected by icicle-covered archways. Killer whales gathered in clumps, and thousands of mermaids swam the streets as loud clangs and beeps and voices flooded the water around them.

'IT'S LOUD, ISN'T IT?!' Gronnyupple yelled into a killer whale's face.

Over near the parked clam car, there was a problem.

'So … it turns out,' Zelda said slowly, 'Gillica is a world-famous ice-skating mermaid who dresses as a seal called Blubble.'

The guards edged forward for her autograph.

'Here's your costume!' a security mermaid said, placing a rubbery fake-seal costume in Zelda's arms.

'Thank you for sending it ahead of your arrival. It's all security checked and ready to go.'

Zelda squeezed it and it began to play a little jingle.

She skates, she glides, she moves from side to side.
She's big and she's trouble,
Yeah … she's Blubble.

Zelda forced a smile.

Beattie couldn't help but laugh. But it came out in slow motion, because her lips were almost frozen shut.

'Now,' the other guard said, 'you'll want to see the stage we've set up for the Blubble show.'

Zelda sneakily pulled a map from the guard's pocket and handed it to Beattie.

'We'll have to escort you to the stage, of course,' the guard went on. 'You aren't allowed out of the Glisten Quarter.'

'We need to lose them,' Zelda whispered to Beattie.

'I beg your pardon?' the guards said at the same time.

'Your beg is pardoned,' Mimi answered, bowing.

The guards exchanged confused looks. 'Out-of-towners,' one mumbled to the other. 'Stay there, and we'll load up the whales with the extra kit we need for the stage. I hear you're going to be jump-skating through hoops.' The guard pointed over to a shark wearing a wig. 'And what is the wigged shark going to do?'

Zelda stared blankly at the shark.

'That would be ... telling,' she said.

As soon as the guards swam off, everyone huddled around the map.

'Where to?' Zelda said. 'We need to decide quickly.'

Frostopia was laid out like a lopsided snowflake split into four uneven quarters – Slushville, Flurry Falls, Floe and the Glisten Quarter. But Beattie saw there was something strange about the map – Slushville and Flurry Falls were separated from Floe and the Glisten Quarter by a huge underwater waterfall. One side said South Pole, the other said North Pole.

'Woah,' Beattie whispered. 'Half of it is on the other

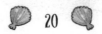

20

FROSTOPIA
SLUSHVILLE
THE GLISTEN QUARTER
SOUTH POLE
NORTH POLE
FLURRY FALLS
FLOE

side of the world! The waterfall must be a magical portal!'

'We expanded to the North Pole thousands of years ago,' a mermaid said as she swam past. 'You can only get into Frostopia from the South Pole waters, but once inside, you can use the underwater waterfall to take you to the north.'

They stared eagerly at the map.

'I like the look of Flurry Falls,' Paris whispered.

'Slushville,' Zelda said with an approving nod. 'Then we'd get to go through the waterfall.'

'*Floe!*' Mimi sang as she swam around their heads and slapped the top left of the map.

'Slushville is a paradise,' Steve read aloud, moving his snout along the text descriptions on the map. 'Full of shops and fun. Floe is a little village, but it's got the funniest mermaids in town. Flurry Falls is a bit mysterious – it just says "Strange things happen in Flurry Falls."'

Steve spun round. 'Slushville. We're going shopping in Slushville.'

'But we have to stay inside the Glisten Quarter,' Beattie whispered back.

'Only if you're Gillica,' Steve pointed out. 'But we're not Gillica. We're not even meant to be here at all.'

'There's no time for shopping,' Gronnyupple said. 'We need to find Maritza Mist before we do anything. She's in danger, I just know it. She didn't deliver my catalogue order, and those water witches who escaped from Viperview Prison have probably got her by now!'

'We don't know that the two are even linked yet,' Beattie said, trying to comfort her.

'And how do you know Maritza Mist isn't in Slushville? In a shop?' Steve said.

Gronnyupple stopped chewing her Seahorse Surprise. 'I don't, actually. Let's go to a shop in Slushville!'

'Can we go quickly?' Zelda groaned, her teeth chattering. Frost had spread across her tail and was mushrooming from her hair.

Beattie snapped an icicle off her nose. 'Steve's right – we can't save Maritza Mist if we're frozen. A quick stop

to pick up something warm to wear – and then we go and find her.'

'Where will we get the money to pay for new clothes?' Paris asked as the guard returned for another of Gillica's trunks.

'Oh, and here's your fee,' the guard said. He handed Zelda a frozen box full of Frosties, Frostopian money.

'Well, that was easy,' Beattie mumbled as Zelda filled her waistcoat pockets.

They waved as the guard swam off again.

'WE'LL BE WAITING RIGHT HERE,' Zelda lied. 'WE'RE NOT GOING *ANYWHERE*.'

4

The Magic of Mermaid Rockits

Sabrina the seahorse taught most of Meri's spy-school lessons in Fortress Bay. She was loud, despite her size, and had once famously wrestled a whale and won.

'ROCKITS!' Sabrina roared as sparkly rocks covered in mermaid scales landed in front of each of the students. 'Who can tell me what they do? Meri?'

The Teenies rolled their eyes in unison. The Teenies were triplet mermaids and Meri's sunken bunkmates. They said the same thing and did the same thing at the same time, always.

Meri cleared her throat and tried to steady her voice. It was difficult to act normal with the ice narwhal missing, especially as it was Sabrina who had secretly tasked her with looking after it. 'Rockits are the latest in virtual spy technology. The rocklike device links up

with your tail, so not only can you see scenes from around the world, you can swim *within* them, as if you're really there.'

'Your voice is weird today,' Sabrina said, swimming closer.

'Your ... face is weird today,' Meri joked awkwardly.

Sabrina hovered so close Meri went cross-eyed.

'You're wrong about my face, but you're completely correct about the Rockits,' Sabrina said. 'Now, let's see what you can all do with one, shall we?'

As soon as Meri clasped the cold rock in her hand, she knew where she wanted to go. She swished her tail until it showed the route of her telephone fish. Then she held the Rockit out in front of her and – *swoosh*.

Everything looked a little see-through and fake, but she was there, swimming towards the ice walls of Frostopia next to the little fish. It morphed as it got closer, switching colour and size to resemble a Frostopia fish, and wriggled through a small crack in the wall. Meri, being in virtual reality, glided right through beside it, but something made her stop.

A couple of mermaids were tunnelling through the wall using what she knew to be a rare water-witch Melt potion. They looked familiar.

Three coughs hit her ear, along with a prod. She dropped the rock and was back in the classroom, swimming against the ceiling, her tail flipping at speed.

'Show-off,' the Teenies all said at once.

'What did you see?' Sabrina asked eagerly. 'You looked like you were surprised.'

Meri swam back to her workstation. 'Nothing,' she said quickly. 'My Rockit didn't work.'

'Why is she even in spy school?' the Teenies chorused, circling around Meri with matching smirks.

'WHY ARE *YOU THREE* HERE?!' Meri shouted

back. 'YOU'RE … THREE TIMES MORE LIKELY TO GET CAUGHT SPYING!'

'Good comeback,' the Teenies said sarcastically. 'Triplet jokes – so creative.'

'Meri was destined to come here because she was born with the spy tail,' Sabrina butted in, prodding each of them with her nose. 'And you triplets might prove useful. It's handy to have three identical mermaids.'

'BUT WE'RE SO DIFFERENT,' the Teenies said.

Sabrina sighed. 'We'll leave it here for today. Take your Rockits and practise. We'll try again tomorrow.'

The trainee spies swam out into the corridor, where spy whales and students floated before their next class.

Meri hung back until the coast was clear, then she fired up the Rockit again.

The mermaids were still there, tunnelling through the wall. She swam closer to get a better look at their faces, and saw something that made her drop the Rockit in shock.

'The ice narwhal,' she whispered to Lady Wriggles. 'They've got the ice narwhal!'

5

Slushville Is So Slush

Back in Frostopia, Beattie parked the clam car and dived through the icy underwater waterfall to the North Pole. They landed in Slushville, where everything was slushy, and the reason it was slushy was because it was home to *a lot* of seals. Mermaids with frozen tails and fluffy hats barged past Beattie and disappeared down the sloppy streets.

'Shopping time!' Steve cheered.

'Look at everyone's tails,' Paris said as they weaved their way through the slush and the crowds. 'They're almost all the same – black with splodges of white, just like the killer whales!'

Beattie worried their tails would be an instant giveaway that they weren't from Frostopia, but every so often a mermaid with a blue tail or a pink or

purple one would swim past too.

Zelda dodged seals like the professional shockey mermaid she was. She stopped and leaned arrogantly against one of them. 'Hurry up, slowmaids!'

'Um, Zelda,' Mimi said, 'that seal says, and I quote, "If you continue to touch me, I will kill you."'

Zelda shot the seal a nervous look before backing off. 'It's a good thing you're a fishtalker, Mimi.'

'I can see more seals than sea!' Paris cried. She shook her necklace and morphed into a jellyfish, hoping that being significantly smaller would help with the navigating, but she seized up and her little jellyfish stingers froze.

'Ah,' Mimi said, picking her up before she sank. 'Paris is telling me in Jellyfish language that she's too frozen to make her necklace work.' She gave it a shake and Paris, with a *FLLLISSSSPIP*, morphed into a shark.

The seals scattered.

'Perfect,' Beattie said as Paris cleared a path for them.

They glided through town, past a mermaid with a tall fur hat who called, 'Welcome to Slushville! Head to Polar Peaks for half-price Icetipple!'

Above them, Beattie could see lots of holes in the ice ceiling.

All around them, mermaids flopped into gondolas pulled by seals and then shot up through the holes. Beattie could see that each of the holes had a dancing hologram next to it – there was a polar bear hologram holding a sign that read *POLAR PEAKS*, and a smiling mermaid hologram with a T-shirt that said *GLAMBEY'S FROZEN FASHION*.

'*That's* where we need to go,' Steve said, spotting the word 'fashion'.

A seal pulling a large gondola lolloped up to Beattie. They all got in, apart from Paris, in shark form, who put a fin in the boat. The seal barked. Everyone stopped dead in their tracks and stared.

Another seal nodded madly at a sign: *WE'LL TRANSPORT ANYTHING THAT DOESN'T EAT US.*

'I won't eat you!' Paris cried, but it came out as 'Gnash, gnash, gnash!'

She shook the necklace with her teeth and morphed into a mermaid. 'Better?' she asked.

The seal nodded.

'To Glambey's Frozen Fashion!' Steve shouted, and the seal glided off towards the hole in the ice above them.

'Welcome to GLAMBEY'S FROZEN FASHION!' the hologram greeted them as they shot through and skidded into an icy cave.

'We're above water!' Zelda yelled, punching the air. 'We're in human territory. Wait – is this dangerous? Because danger is my middle name!'

'No it's not, it's Pamela,' Mimi reminded her.

'It's very safe,' a mermaid said as she slid next to them in another gondola. 'Humans don't come this deep into the ice. You're at the top of the world!'

Beattie excitedly leaned forward in the gondola as they careered towards ice rails filled with furry tops and glistening tail embellishments. Up ahead, mermaids pulled by seals plucked items off the shelves – hats and gloves and little icy bags. Over at the changing rooms, a mermaid wearing a sparkling waistcoat slipped out from behind the frost-covered curtains.

'I want something like that!' Zelda said. 'I love a waistcoat.'

'We're here to get *warm* things,' Steve protested, dipping his head in a puddle at the bottom of the gondola. Unlike mermaids and seals, Steve couldn't breathe out of water.

Zelda stuck her tongue out at him. 'I'm getting the waistcoat.'

Beattie shivered and pulled a coat with a fluffy trim from the racks. Frostopia was *cool*.

Mimi chose a T-shirt with a half penguin, half hamburger on it.

'That's my favourite cartoon!' a young mermaid called as she shot past.

'That's weird – I instantly feel much warmer,' Mimi said.

'Everything in this shop will keep you warm,' the shop owner said as she slid past on a seal.

'You need to get this, Paris,' Steve said, holding up a furry crown.

'Do you think it might be a bit much?' Paris asked, reluctantly putting it on.

'Absolutely not,' Steve said. 'If anything, it's not enough. Now we just need something for Gronnyupple.'

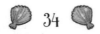

Beattie spotted her in the corner of the shop, belly up, putting the Blubble seal costume on a passing seal – and laughing hysterically.

'Gronnyupple!' Zelda shouted. 'WHAT ARE YOU DOING?'

The seal got a fright and flopped out of the shop, still wearing the costume.

Beattie shuffled over and peered down through the hole. 'If the guards find us outside of the Glisten Quarter *and* we've lost the Blubble costume … Oh cods, this isn't good.'

'I love Blubble!' an ancient-looking mermaid said as she swam past with a gondola full of hats.

'It's fine!' Gronnyupple said. 'We'll easily find it. It's a seal dressed up as a … Ah, I see what I've done.'

Steve shook his head. 'This is not turning out to be the successful shopping trip I wanted!'

Gronnyupple bit her lip. 'Sorry, I just thought the seal would look great dressed like—'

'A seal,' Steve finished.

'We could say we misplaced the costume?'

Gronnyupple suggested. 'Or we could say a killer whale ate it?'

A killer whale popped its head through the hole.

'He says you really need to stop with that stereotype,' Mimi said. 'Killer whales don't eat everything. They don't even like being called killer whales. They actually prefer "deluxe dolphins".'

'*Wait*,' Gronnyupple said, sniffing the air. 'I smell a water witch.'

'Is it Beattie?' Zelda said flatly.

Beattie's eyes widened. She could smell it too! It smelled like the candyfloss humans ate, only a bit burned and soggy.

Gronnyupple pulled at Zelda's waistcoat, sniffing it excitedly.

'Get off!' Zelda cried. But Gronnyupple was already peeling the waistcoat from her back.

She held it up and pointed at the label.

'Made by MM,' Beattie read.

'Maritza Mist!' Gronnyupple cried. 'It's got to be her! How many people have the initials MM?'

'Marjorie Mussels, Max Mako, Martina Mackerel, Moya von Manatee,' Steve listed. 'Molly Marine, Mairie Mul—'

'*Exactly,*' Gronnyupple interrupted. 'Almost *no one*. I bet it's her, and that the shop owner knows where we can find her!'

They all cheered! And then a goblin shark came crashing into the shop and grabbed Gronnyupple's tail in its teeth.

6

Simoseal

The goblin shark refused to let Gronnyupple go. It was a strange-looking shark, covered in amber jewels, with twinkling amber eyes – certainly not the kind of shark that looked as though it belonged in Frostopia.

'Looks like you're the Seahorse Surprise sweet now,' Steve joked.

'STEVE!' Beattie shouted. 'So inappropriate.'

'LET HER GO,' Paris demanded, but the goblin shark shook its head.

'Seriously,' Zelda said, buttoning up her waistcoat in anticipation of a chase. 'LET THE MERMAID GO.'

The shark took one look at Zelda and dived through the icy floor, shattering it into tiny shards!

Beattie tumbled back into the water, surrounded by clumps of clothes and screaming mermaids.

'GRONNYUPPLE!' she cried. 'GRONNYUPPLE!'

'You find Maritza … I'll handle this,' Paris said, and with a *FLIIISSSIP* she morphed into a shark and tore after Gronnyupple.

'Excuse me,' came Steve's voice from where the shop owner had landed, face first on the back of a polar bear. 'Not a good time to ask, I realise – but do you happen to know where the designer of these clothes lives?'

'Mee met mem melivered my meal,' the mermaid mumbled through the polar bear's fluff.

Steve turned to the others. 'THEY GET THEM DELIVERED BY SEAL! Mimi, work your magic!'

'Thank you for the clothes,' Beattie said, placing some Frosties sheepishly next to the shop owner's smooshed face.

Mimi swam from seal to seal, asking if they could help.

'THIS ONE SAYS HER NAME IS SUSASEAL, BUT I NEED TO FIND SIMOSEAL. HE'S THE ONE WE NEED.'

They looked around at the hundreds of seals pulling their gondolas.

'SIMOSEAL?' Beattie shouted hopefully.

A seal came lolloping over. Mimi did the thumbs up.

'Simoseal says he knows where Maritza Mist lives – at 000 Underwater Igloo Avenue, Flurry Falls.'

'You know,' Zelda said, 'I'm jealous of all your powers – Paris can morph and Beattie and Gronnyupple are water witches, but actually, Mimi, I think your fishtalking might be the best!'

'I CAN'T HEAR YOU!' Mimi said to Zelda as a particularly chatty shoal of fish swam past.

They dived into Simoseal's gondola.

'PLEASE TAKE US TO MARITZA MIST!' Zelda shouted.

The seal drop-dived, pinning them all to the back of the gondola.

'I hope we don't lose Paris!' Beattie yelled as her cheeks wobbled madly as they tore through the sea.

When she dared to look down, she saw little igloos being battered by thundering underwater waterfalls. A frozen sign cobbled together from sunken treasure spelled out *FLURRY FALLS*.

'Don't worry, Beattie,' Zelda said. 'Paris will find

Gronnyupple and be back with us in no time. When she's a shark, she has an incredibly powerful sense of smell. She'll pick us up.'

'I hope you're right,' Beattie said with a gulp. 'We can't lose Paris as well.'

7

Meri Does Some Midnight Spying

Meri swam back to her room after a long day. She had struggled to concentrate in her afternoon spy classes. And she barely touched her dinner, even though it was her *favourite* chomp chops, secretly sourced from Jawella's, the shark restaurant in Hammerhead Heights in the Hidden Lagoon.

'Not like you to not eat your chomp chops,' the Teenies said.

'I wasn't hungry,' Meri said, flopping on to her top bunk.

The Teenies floated up beside her.

Meri rolled over, pulled out her seaweed notebook from under her seaweed pillow and began scribbling in it, keeping one eye on her tail.

'You're looking at your tail, but you're not meant

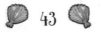

to spy out of hours,' the Teenies said. 'Who are you spying on?'

'No one,' Meri said. 'I was just admiring how slimy my scales look today.'

The Teenies retreated to their bunk – an extra wide one so they could sleep side by side. But Meri could tell they weren't convinced.

She watched scene after scene of Frostopia swimways and houses and shops and igloos, but she couldn't see the mermaids with the ice narwhal.

'Where are you?' she whispered to her tail.

She waited until she heard the Teenies snoring in unison, and then pulled out her clamshell compact. On the shell's hidden screen, she scrolled through pictures of mermaids on the most-wanted list, until she found them.

'The escaped Viperview mermaids,' she muttered to herself, writing their names in her notebook: *Gulper and Rose Rockweed*.

She read the report that accompanied their pictures. A human called Susan Silkensocks had damaged

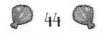

Viperview Prison with a ship and they had escaped with a mermaid called Ommy, who was captured instantly when he swam into a rock and knocked himself out.

Meri gasped and shook her head when she read the next line: '*Gulper and Rose Rockweed found and returned to Viperview. Case closed.*'

'But they aren't in Viperview,' Meri said, floating off her bunk and hitting the ceiling. 'They're breaking into Frostopia!'

'MERI! GO TO SLEEP!' the Teenies shouted, before immediately snoring again.

Meri sneak-swam to the door. She needed to tell Sabrina the mermaids hadn't been caught – they were free and dangerous. But she wouldn't mention the ice narwhal thing. Not yet. Maybe she could convince Sabrina to let her go on her first real mission to capture the Viperview mermaids. And then she could sneakily get the ice narwhal and put it back before anyone noticed.

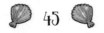

'GO TO SLEEP, MERI!' Sabrina shouted. 'The Rockweeds have been caught. Everything is under control.'

'But I saw them,' Meri said, swimming around the outside of Sabrina's tiny bejewelled house.

'Impossible,' Sabrina said. 'I'll show you on your tail – look, that's them in Viperview Prison.'

Meri stared at her tail in disbelief. It was true, they were in Viperview. 'But … I'm *certain* it was them.'

A roll of seaweed floated towards her.

'The capture notes,' Sabrina said. 'We interviewed them after they were caught. As you can see, nothing out of the ordinary.'

SPY TT 202: Gulper. Rose. What's your favourite thing to do?

Rose: Knitting.

Gulper: Plotting evil things.

SPY TT 202: Fascinating! Do you knit with sunken wool, and what kind of evil things do you plot?

 46

Rose: Nope. Hair.

Gulper: Destroy the world. FISH EYE!

A delightful interview! Thank you to Gulper and Rose. CONFIRM: It is Gulper and Rose. CASE CLOSED.

'What does Fish Eye mean?' Meri asked. 'Gulper said FISH EYE.'

'It's the things that fish have on their faces,' Sabrina explained. 'Along with lips and … Do they have noses? Look, Meri, if this is a silly attempt to get out of Fortress Bay and go on a mission, it is definitely not working.'

Meri slumped. 'I just thought I could—'

'GO TO BED, MERI,' Sabrina said firmly. 'That's enough now. Don't make me call Lady Wriggles.'

Lady Wriggles was both an assistant and a nightmare if you interrupted her beauty sleep. The last thing Meri needed was an angry jellyfish stinging her. *Swim Together, Sink Together.* If Meri was in trouble with a teacher, then so was Lady Wriggles.

'Fine,' Meri huffed. 'But you're wrong, Sabrina! I know

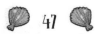

what I saw!' She swam off towards the dorms, watching her tail as she went. She could see a bunch of guards swimming furiously through the streets of Frostopia, waving a CATCH GILLICA THE ICE-SKATING SEAL poster. The imagery switched to Flurry Falls just as Meri reached the empty canteen. She grabbed a chomp chop and munched on it, trying to think.

A mermaid with a flick of green hair slid into view on her tail. She was in a gondola with two other mermaids. Meri sighed at the sight of them – 'Oh to have friends!'

They didn't look like they were having fun as they were pulled through the icy waters by a seal at break-neck speed, but still.

Meri wiped the chomp chop juice from her lips and pulled out her clamshell compact. She scanned it against the mermaids on her tail.

MERMAIDS FROM THE HIDDEN LAGOON.
POTENTIALLY BAD MERMAIDS IN FORBIDDEN
TERRITORY.
ENTRY OCCURRED THIS MORNING.

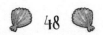

ALERT OUT IN FROSTOPIA FOR THEIR CAPTURE —
SEAL COSTUME INCIDENT.
UNDER CONTROL, NO FORTRESS BAY
INVOLVEMENT NEEDED.

'Why are you so far from home?' Meri muttered.

A guilty-looking whale emerged from the kitchen and swam away sheepishly. He was clearly having a midnight snack.

'I didn't mean you!' Meri called after him. She chewed on her chomp chop again as she read through the profiles. She stopped when she got to Mimi's.

'A fishtalker, eh?' An idea came to her. 'Well, if I can't get out of here, maybe Mimi can help me get the ice narwhal back ...'

She pressed the FISHTALKER TALK button on her clamshell compact and took a deep breath.

8

Underwater Igloo Avenue, Flurry Falls

Hundreds of icicle-covered arches glistened for as far as Beattie could see. Fast-flowing waterfalls broke through from the surface and landed in icy pools, where hundreds of mermaids lazed and drank Icetipple. Killer whales floated around, and above them Beattie could see baby mermaids taking swimming lessons with polar bear cubs.

Mimi looked around in wide-eyed wonder as they soared past in the gondola.

'Beautiful, isn't it?' Beattie said wistfully.

'Every single sea creature is shouting that they're merry,' Mimi chirped. 'Is that nice or weird?'

'Merry?' Zelda said.

'I AM MERI! CAN YOU HEAR ME?' a group of polar bear cubs shouted.

 50

'I AM MERI!' a whale bellowed.

A fish turned to her and screamed, 'I AM MERI!'

Mimi turned round in the gondola, her mouth hanging open.

'Mimi?' Zelda said, nudging her. 'Everything all right?'

'Yes …' she answered finally. 'This place is wonderful, every creature is so MERRY!'

Far away in Fortress Bay, Meri Pebble hit her head against a desk.

The seal weaved through the frozen arches before coming to a halt outside a small igloo. The initials MM were carved next to the frozen door.

'Maritza Mist's house,' Beattie said.

She reached out to knock, then turned to the others. 'What if she's … dangerous?'

Zelda rolled her eyes. 'She's some old mermaid who makes magic for a catalogue. I think we'll live.'

She swam past Beattie and knocked for her.

The door creaked open.

'Hello?' Beattie whispered as they swam inside. It was a tiny igloo with only a couple of doors leading to other rooms and some sunken human paintings hanging lop-sided on the wall.

They heard a creak and a swish of a tail coming from the next room. Something clattered and the door flew open!

'Maritza?' Beattie said hopefully.

It was indeed Maritza Mist. But she was not what they were expecting. Not what they were expecting *at all*.

9

Meri Screams I AM MERI, a Lot

'How many times do I have to scream "I AM MERI" before this Mimi mermaid realises that all the sea creatures aren't *merry*? I'm trying to tell her I AM MERI and I AM TRYING TO CONTACT HER! What's the point of this *use any creature to deliver a message to a fishtalker* technology if the mermaid DOESN'T GET IT?!'

She took a deep breath as she watched her tail – a fish swam past Mimi's nose. 'I AM MERI!' she shouted again.

'We *know*,' the Teenies said.

Meri froze and tried to act casual as they floated past with their canteen trays. She wasn't sure how long they'd been there. The canteen was full and she hadn't even noticed – it was Sandcrackle cereal time already.

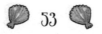

'I AM MERI!' Meri tried again.

Lady Wriggles thrust a piece of seaweed in her face.

TRY CHANGING YOUR NAME TO GORDON.

'Lady Wriggles,' Meri said. 'You're a *genius*.'

10

Maritza Mist

Beattie floated in silence, staring at the mermaid Gronnyupple believed to be the most powerful water witch in the world.

She had icy hair pulled into three neat buns, and a small black and white splodged tail. She was wearing a Burguin T-shirt, just like Mimi.

'She's about seven years old,' Zelda whispered to Beattie out of the corner of her mouth. She turned to Mimi and mouthed, 'SEVEN.'

Maritza Mist's ear grew bigger. 'Listening spell, dears,' she said, pointing at it. 'It's a new creation of mine. Oh, and I am actually exceedingly old. But I smeared my tail in immortality paste when I was seven, so now I'm immortal and stuck looking like this forever. It's why I sound like a granny, dears, but I look like you.'

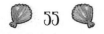 55

Beattie and the others rolled back on their tails in fits of relieved giggles.

'Why did you cover your tail in immortality paste?' Beattie asked when she'd stopped laughing.

'Because I have to try out my spells first, dear. I can't just sell any old thing! Now, answer me this – why are you here?'

'Well, at first we wanted to come because you didn't deliver a catalogue order to the Crocodile Kingdom,' Beattie said.

'That's a long way to come to complain about tardy deliveries.'

'No, it's not a complaint – Gronnyupple thought something had happened to you,' Zelda explained. 'But you're *immortal* and indestructible! She'll be so relieved.'

'Oh poor Gronnyupple. I was just a little delayed because I wanted to throw in a free listening spell for her as a surprise! Why isn't she here?'

Beattie tried to think of the best way to phrase the goblin shark situation.

'Goblin shark,' Mimi chirped, 'which is not ideal, but she'll be happy to know you're safe – she was convinced the immortal mermaids who escaped from Viperview had got you and that's why you didn't deliver the catalogue order.'

Maritza's face fell. 'They escaped from Viperview?'

Before Mimi could reply, the door flew open. They ducked for cover as frozen splinters rained down on them.

Two mermaids floated in with orange and black-scaled tails and smug grins.

'Maritza?' Beattie asked. 'Who are these mermaids?' She could tell by the way they were all staring at each other that they weren't friends.

'Why, it's Gulper and Rose Rockweed. How did you escape from Viperview?' Maritza asked.

'*WELL*—' Rose Rockweed began, but a fish interrupted her.

It was tiny and exhausted and swam through the door, spewing bubbles that rearranged themselves into letters.

CODE BLUE ... CODE BL ... U ... E. Urgent ...

message ... to ... be ... delivered ... to ... Maritza ...
Mist ... of ... Realm ... Nine ... Frostopia ... The ...
ice ... narwhal ... is GONE.

Rose Rockweed threw her arms in the air. 'Well, that ruined my big speech – I've been practising it all the way here! It's true, we have the ice narwhal!'

Beattie could have sworn Maritza Mist's eyes flashed with panic, but she floated like a mermaid who had everything under control.

Rose shoved a small icy sculpture in Maritza's face. '*And* we got the list of where you hid the rest of them. They just leave these things lying around in Fortress Bay,' she laughed. 'It's too easy.'

'What's an ice narwhal?' Beattie asked, but Maritza Mist didn't answer.

'Very good, Rockweeds,' she said. 'But why are you here?'

Gulper and Rose began swimming in threatening circles. 'To stock up on magic, of course! We have a lot to do and we need some of your potions to help us.'

'It's time for you to go, dears,' Maritza said quickly

to the others, as a bunch of seals appeared with a *pop* and began shoving them out of the doorway.

'Why are the seals shoving us outside?' Beattie asked, trying to fight her way back in.

'SEAL POP,' Maritza said knowingly, waving an empty bottle. 'Tell Gronnyupple I'll put one in her next order. Now, off you go.'

'Oh,' Mimi said. 'They're all called Gordon! And one is called Lady Wriggles It's Not Working. That's a long name.'

The seals lined up outside like blubbery bouncers.

There was no way in.

The four mermaids and Steve swam around the side of the igloo and crammed together at the window, watching helplessly as Gulper and Rose began ransacking the place.

'GIVE US YOUR POTIONS!' they yelled.

Spare seals went flying. Ice shattered. Maritza Mist began throwing potions willy-nilly.

One landed on Rose's head and made it swell to the size of a polar bear.

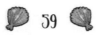

'She's going to pop!' Zelda cried, just as Rose's head deflated like a balloon and sagged on to her shoulders.

'Is she dead?' Mimi whispered.

'They're immortal,' Beattie said. 'This could go on for a while.'

Gulper grabbed Maritza Mist by the tail and flung her across the room. 'YOU CAN'T STOP US!' he yelled.

Maritza landed on a freeze potion. She tried to flick her tail, but the end was frozen solid and she began to sink. 'Drats, that's going to take a few minutes to wear off.'

'MOVE!' Rose shouted to Gulper as she threw another potion at Maritza. But he was too busy laughing.

The potion hit him square in the face and his ears began to droop until his earlobes were as long as his body.

'WHY DOES EVERYTHING SOUND LOOOONG?' he cried.

Maritza Mist cackled as Rose sneaked up behind her and began smearing a strange magical paste over her arms.

'No!' Maritza cried. 'Not—'

All the objects in the room came flying towards her.

'The magnet potion,' she finished with a sigh. She tried to swim, but she was well and truly sunk.

'Let's go to Pinkly Lagoon and get the next ice creature,' Rose said as Gulper grabbed fistfuls of potions and headed for the door. 'SOON EVERY MERMAID KINGDOM IN THE WORLD WILL BE OURS!'

He flicked a potion at the wall.

'Duck!' Beattie cried as the wall exploded.

They watched as Gulper and Rose danced off into the distance.

'Maritza,' Beattie said, hurrying inside. 'Are you all right?'

Maritza Mist cackled. 'Of course I am! That's the problem. I'm immortal, and unfortunately so are Gulper and Rose. And that makes them unstoppable. The mermaid world is about to fall into very bad hands and I fear we are doomed.'

'Doomed?' Beattie whispered nervously.

Maritza Mist smeared a potion on her lips and they magically extended into a megaphone. 'DOOMED, DEARS.'

11

Multistorey Clam-Car Car Park (Say It Fast)

Back in Fortress Bay, Meri had decided that there was only one thing for it – if she was going to fix this mess and get the ice narwhal back, she was going to have to do it herself. Changing her name to Gordon was not going to cut it.

'And that means WE'RE SNEAKING OUT OF HERE!' she said to a wildly unenthusiastic Lady Wriggles.

Meri swam through the multistorey clam car car park and chose a ride. She picked the clam car's lock and the roof flipped open.

'Easy,' she said, while Lady Wriggles hid her eyes with her stinger.

The place was completely empty, apart from the Teenies, whose job it was to guard the cars. But, like

always, they were huddled in the far corner, reading identical copies of *SPY TWEEN* magazine.

Meri began punching buttons on the gem-studded control panel above her head. She'd chosen the clam car with special spy features, including camouflage mode.

'I know what you're thinking,' Meri said, as Lady Wriggles looked at her with her unchanging jellyfish face. 'How are we going to get past the Teenies?'

Lady Wriggles wasn't thinking that – even three small rocks would be harder to get past than the Teenies.

'But I have a plan!' Meri said proudly as she steered the car towards the exit. 'Engage camouflage mode!'

Lady Wriggles could hear Meri's heart beating like a manic octopus. After all, Meri had only seen the outside world on her tail – she'd never actually left Fortress Bay before.

'I hope this works,' she whispered as the clam car inched slowly past the Teenies.

Almost immediately, they snapped their heads up.

'WAIT A *MINUTE*,' the three of them said.

Meri held her breath.

'ACCORDING TO *SPY TWEEN*, ROCKITS ARE THE NEW COOL SPY GADGET THIS SEASON. CAN YOU BELIEVE SABRINA MIGHT ACTUALLY BE COOL? THAT'S BLOWN MY TINY FISHY MIND!'

Meri continued to hold her breath as they drove slowly through the sand security perimeter and out of Fortress Bay.

'We did it!' Meri squealed as soon as they were out of earshot. 'Maybe I'll meet those mermaids from the Hidden Lagoon in Frostopia. It would be nice to make some friends.'

Lady Wriggles turned on the radio and the Squid Sisters started blaring from the speakers.

'You're right,' Meri said with a sad smile. 'Spy mermaids can't have friends.'

12

Wartina's Necklace

'Now, I'm very sorry, dears, but I have a few things to do,' Maritza said as she swam towards the door at the back of her igloo.

'Things to do with the ice narwhal?' Beattie guessed.

Maritza Mist stopped.

'It's safer if you don't get involved.'

'We could help,' Beattie said. 'We're excellent at stopping disasters.'

'And at causing them,' Zelda whispered to Mimi.

'Are you good or bad mermaids?' Maritza asked.

Beattie beamed. 'Good ones. Definitely.'

'Depends who you ask,' Zelda mumbled.

Maritza made her way through the door and into a cluttered room beyond.

They followed.

Potion bottles floated about their heads, while a polar bear in the corner folded catalogues by sitting on them.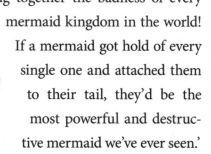

'I created one ice creature for every mermaid kingdom around the world, and Frostopia's was the ice narwhal. Each one contained a little sprinkle of good potion to encourage unity – mermaids of the world united! But I had a friend named Wartina Brittle who sneakily switched the potions, making the ice creatures *very bad* – so the potion within them caused division and destruction instead. And what made it worse was that when combined they'd bring together the badness of every mermaid kingdom in the world!

If a mermaid got hold of every single one and attached them to their tail, they'd be the most powerful and destructive mermaid we've ever seen.'

'Did Wartina use them?' Beattie asked. 'Did she become all-powerful?'

'Almost,' Maritza Mist explained, 'but I managed to stop her. The problem was I couldn't do anything about the magic within the ice creatures. All I could do was hide them far away from each other to limit their power. Though the damage had been done – they divided and destroyed the bonds between many mermaids. And as the years passed, mermaids in different realms no longer spoke to one another. Some still speak to or visit one another, but it's not like it used to be. They built ice walls and hidden cities, until realms like your Hidden Lagoon forgot about their other mermaid friends and believed places like the Crocodile Kingdom to be nothing but a myth.'

'Wartina doesn't sound like a very nice friend,' Mimi said. 'But I *really* like her name.'

'So Gulper and Rose want

that magic now. They want to become all-powerful,' Beattie said. 'We can't let that happen!'

'What about trying to remove the immortality-paste spell? Then Gulper and Rose would be gone forever,' Zelda suggested.

Maritza Mist shook her head. 'Reversing or removing a spell can only be done with Razzle Dazzle kelp, and it would be a *miracle* if we found any.'

'How can you tell if it's Razzle Dazzle kelp?' Beattie asked.

Maritza Mist smiled. 'It's always showing off.'

'SOUNDS LIKE MY KIND OF KELP!' Steve joked.

'It's impossible to find,' Maritza Mist said sadly. 'Believe me, I've looked. It would be nice to undo this immortality spell on me too.'

'So Gulper and Rose are going to try to collect all the ice creatures,' Beattie said.

Maritza Mist nodded gravely. 'They already have the ice creature from Rainbow Landing – a seahorse. They stole it hundreds of years ago, after they used the

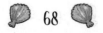

immortality paste. I knew then exactly what they were up to, so I framed them for a crime and got them locked away in Viperview.'

'Let's frame them again!' Zelda said. 'I'll commit a little crime, and then we'll tell everyone it was them.'

'Zelda,' Beattie said, sounding shocked. 'You can't commit a *crime*.'

'You haven't even heard my crime ideas yet,' Zelda said with a pout.

The polar bear in the corner groaned and pointed towards the door – there, floating sadly on the spot, was a familiar figure.

'Paris!' Beattie cried, racing over and hugging her. 'You found us!'

'You used your extra-sensitive shark nose, didn't you?' Zelda said. 'I told everyone that's what you'd do!'

'No,' Paris said. 'I just asked the mermaid in the shop where you were – apparently Mimi shouted out the address really loudly before you left.'

Mimi bowed.

'I lost Gronnyupple,' Paris said with a tear in her eye.

'The goblin shark was too fast. I don't know where she's gone.'

'Oh no,' Beattie said. 'Maybe Maritza can help us find her. She's got a slight problem on her hands with some immortal mermaids who ransacked her igloo and stole potions to help them take over the world, but—'

There was a crash as Maritza tumbled over the polar bear. She was wide-eyed and impossibly pale, like she'd seen a ghost jellyfish.

'Maritza?' Beattie whispered.

'That necklace,' Maritza said, choking out the words as if they were frozen in her throat. 'Where did you get it?'

Paris looked down at her necklace. 'It was a present from Arabella Cod, the mermaid queen of the Hidden Lagoon. She gave it to me for saving her life.'

'It's magic,' Zelda said. 'Paris is a human, but with the necklace she can morph into all sorts of sea creatures.'

'There's something I didn't tell you about Wartina Brittle,' Maritza said. 'She was a human … and that was her necklace.'

13

Gronnyupple in Trouble

Far away in Amberberg, where mermaid palaces made of amber wound around the rocks, Gronnyupple was in trouble.

Mermaids and codfish clad in amber jewels floated in the room where the goblin shark had dropped off Gronnyupple.

'SEND HER TO VIPERVIEW!' they shouted. 'FOR ONE HUNDRED YEARS!'

'Can I have some Seahorse Surprise?' Gronnyupple asked. 'Or my backpack full of spells ... I mean SPOILS ... wait, no, that sounds like I've stolen something.'

An old mermaid judge with a luminous orange tail read the seaweed notes in front of him.

'Gronnyupple Wondra Crab, you have been brought

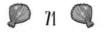

here by goblin shark because you are accused of robbing Amberberg Central Bank and stealing over one million Ambug coins. You also stand accused of robbing the city's crown jewel – the Amber Flubby – and of looting various shops around the city. How do you plead?'

Gronnyupple thought for a second. 'Um, well … it would be something like *pleeeeease! Pleeeeeease!*' She clasped her hands together. 'And my hands would be like this, for extra effect.'

The judge stared down his nose at her.

Another mermaid, with orange hair twisted into a cone shape, swam around Gronnyupple, holding up a packet of Seahorse Surprise.

'This is your calling card. A half-eaten packet of Seahorse Surprise – you leave one at the locations of all your crimes.'

'But lots of mermaids eat Seahorse Surprise.'

The mermaid laughed. 'Indeed, but you *love* Seahorse Surprise, don't you?'

'YES!' Gronnyupple cried, punching the water in triumph. 'But I'd *never* leave them half-eaten. I *always*

finish the packet. I hope when you find the real thief you'll punish them for wasting good sweets.'

'You must prove to us that you are not responsible for these crimes,' the judge said. 'If we don't believe you, then you will be sent to VIPERVIEW PRISON!'

'Do they have Seahorse Surprise there?' Gronnyupple asked hopefully.

14

The Power of Paris

Paris held the crystal pendant of her necklace firmly in her hand. 'Should I, um, take it off?'

'NO!' Beattie, Mimi, Zelda and Maritza all shouted.

'You're a human, remember?' Beattie said. 'If you take the necklace off you'll morph back—'

'And we're miles under the ice!' Zelda finished.

'And humans swim slowly,' Mimi added.

'You must not do that, dear,' Maritza said, swimming around Paris. 'The necklace is yours now. I made it myself!' She stopped and stared, her eyes growing wide. 'You know, Paris might be just what we need to defeat Gulper and Rose forever.'

Paris looked concerned.

'Water-witch magic gets stronger in the hands of a human,' Maritza explained. 'I tell all the water witches

who get my catalogue about the
bad human who nearly destroyed
us all. Gronnyupple knows this
story, or at least the short version of
it. I designed the necklace as a
fishtalker device – the mermaids
who wear it can hear the sea
creatures. But a human who
wears it can *become* those
creatures. When Wartina Brittle
collected and then tried to use the
ice creatures, there was a snag in her
plan – the ice creatures cracked when she
held them. Being a human made the magic too strong for
the ice to contain it. And, of course, if an ice creature
broke—'

'The magic would lose its power, it would be useless,'
Beattie said.

'Exactly,' Maritza said. 'So she went off to find a
mermaid who would help her – someone who could
hold the magic. She ended up convincing Mary Ruster,

who wasn't a bad mermaid at all, just clumsy and very silly with her magic.'

'Her ancient sunken ship is in our lagoon!' Beattie cried. 'Did she succeed in helping Wartina?'

'No,' Maritza said. 'I stopped them with the help of the Fortress Bay mermaids. They gave Wartina an ultimatum – be locked away in Fortress Bay or leave for land and never return. So of course she chose land. She threw that necklace away and I never saw her again. It became known as the morphing necklace among the very few who knew of its existence. And every couple of hundred years a mermaid might hear whispers about it and ask me if I'd made it.

She produced some seaweed letters.

DEAR MARITZA,
DID YOU MAKE THE MORPHING NECKLACE?
FROM KRILKY DRAGONHOLM

I pretend I know nothing. I tell them it's either an ancient magic or made up, and hope they'll forget about

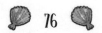

it. So anyway, back to the story. After Wartina was banished, I hid the ice creatures to minimise their power and stop any mermaid trying to use them, and then I sent the ice narwhal and the list of locations to Fortress Bay, and that's where they've been for hundreds of years. Until now.'

'So what you're saying,' Beattie said slowly, 'is that because Wartina was a human, the ice creatures were so powerful they cracked in her hands. So if Paris can get hold of an ice creature—'

'There is a strong possibility she could destroy it,' Maritza Mist finished.

Beattie flicked her tail excitedly. 'And in order for the ice creatures to work, Gulper and Rose need *all* of them. But if we destroy one—'

'You win,' Maritza said.

'Where are they hidden?' Beattie asked eagerly.

'Each mermaid realm has one, though I've forgotten most of the locations now – and Gulper and Rose have the list. Frostopia's is the narwhal, which Gulper and Rose already stole from Fortress Bay. They also have the

ice seahorse from Rainbow Landing – they got that one hundreds of years before they were sent to Viperview. And now they're on their way to Pinkly Lagoon, where I hid an ice leech in the old town of Vampire Rocks.'

'But they have a head start,' Zelda groaned. 'It'll take us ages to get to another kingdom.'

'Well, for that I have one more trick up my sleeve,' Maritza Mist said as she threw on a fur-lined cape. 'Come with me.'

15

Jelly and the Whale Bus

Meri put the clam car on auto-swim and curled up in the back seat for a nap. Lady Wriggles was already asleep, wrapped neatly around the steering wheel. They were in crystal-clear waters, filled with slow-swimming fish.

'*AHOOOHGAH!*'

Meri snapped awake.

'*AHOOOHGAH!*'

'Lady Wriggles,' she whispered. 'What creature makes that noise? I haven't been taught that one.'

'*AHOOOHGAH!*'

Lady Wriggles covered her eyes with her tentacles. She knew what sea creature made that noise.

'Seriously,' Meri said, desperately scanning the data on her tail. 'What makes that—'

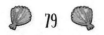

'JELLY HERE! YOU ARE DRIVING IN FORBIDDEN HUMAN TERRITORY. PLEASE BOARD THE WHALE BUS.'

Meri flung herself at the control panel and punched a button. The clam car nestled into the seabed and turned the colour of sand.

'NICE TRY, BUT MY OLD EYES CAN SEE EVERYTHING,' came the voice, as a whale with a sunken human bus on its back floated past the window. A jellyfish with a horn strapped to its head tapped on the windscreen, making Meri and Lady Wriggles jump.

'THIS IS QUENTIN, MY JELLYFISH. HE'LL SHOW YOU WHERE TO PARK YOUR CLAM CAR. YOU'LL GET IT BACK WHEN WE RETURN TO THE LOWER REALMS – SAFE MERMAID TERRITORY. IF YOU RESIST, I WILL SET THE WHALE ON YOU.'

'Great,' Meri groaned.

After she'd parked the clam car on the roof of the bus, Meri wrapped Lady Wriggles in her hair and swam

aboard. She was greeted by a jolly old mermaid with a shrivelled tail.

'How could you see us?' Meri demanded.

Jelly smiled a toothless smile. 'These old eyes see everything … And you forgot to turn your headlights off.'

'Codfuffle,' Meri muttered in frustration.

'Where are you from?' Jelly asked.

'I can't say,' Meri replied quickly.

'Well, you *have* to say,' Jelly said, her smile growing. 'Because now that you're on the bus, I have to take you to safe mermaid territory.'

'Frostopia then,' Meri said.

'You sneaking in?' Jelly asked hopefully.

Meri shook her head.

'That's a shame,' Jelly said. 'I like rebels.'

Meri looked into the almost empty bus. There was only an old man and old lady mermaid on board. And a shopping trolley.

'They're always trying to go for holidays on land with the humans,' Jelly whispered, rolling her eyes. 'In a shopping trolley.'

The mermaids were wearing matching T-shirts that read, *I WENT ON A HUMAN ROLLERCOASTER IN A SHOPPING TROLLEY AND ALL I GOT WAS THIS EXCELLENT T-SHIRT (and a fine).*

'This is going to be a long ride,' Meri whispered to Lady Wriggles.

16

Realm Reach

Beattie and the others followed Maritza Mist through the icicle-covered alleyways of Flurry Falls, and came to a stop at a towering ice wall.

'Dead end,' Zelda said, turning to leave.

'No,' Beattie whispered, running her hand over the ice. 'There's something in there.'

They looked up and gasped – frozen within the wall were a dozen colourful sea creatures.

'THERE'S A SEAHORSE!' Steve wailed, fake-fainting on to Beattie's palm.

Maritza took a deep breath and held her hands up to the wall. She turned to Beattie. 'Do the same – you can make magic, can't you?'

Beattie nearly tumbled back on her tail. She had no idea how Maritza could possibly know that. When

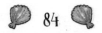

Beattie had first met Gronnyupple, she had used water-witch potions from Maritza's catalogue. But as time went on, Beattie realised she could make the magic herself, though she wasn't very good at it yet.

'You know, dear,' Maritza said, steadying her splodged tail. 'There's usually only one water witch in the world who can make magic. She or he creates the potions for the catalogue and sends them out to all the water witches.'

'But you can also make magic,' Beattie said slowly. 'So that means there's two of us.'

Maritza smiled. 'I know, dear – isn't it strange! There's only meant to be one. They always have and always will run the catalogue – it's their *destiny*. But now there's two of us. It's probably because I'm immortal and not meant to be here. Anyway, what's important now is that you help me reactivate this wall.'

Zelda backed away, pulling Mimi and Paris with her.

Steve looked wide-eyed from Beattie to the wall.

The water was eerily quiet and Beattie could hear what sounded like a dripping tap. She raised her hands,

and glittering water began gushing down the frozen wall, sweeping her friends sideways.

'KEEP GOING!' Maritza shouted as the creatures in the wall began to emerge – sculpted replicas made of colourful ice.

'Oh good,' Steve said. 'They're not real creatures – they'd be so cold!'

'Perfect,' Maritza said, clapping her hands. 'Not bad, Beattie, not bad at all.'

'What is this?' Zelda said, swimming up to the icy inky-coloured octopus on the wall. She reached out a hand.

'CAREFUL!' Maritza shouted, but it was too late. The octopus began swirling around and around until it wasn't an octopus any more but a dark watery opening in the wall.

'Cool!' Zelda cried, pushing her whole head in. She reeled back in shock. 'It's Octopolli in there! The realm where the mermaids have octopus tentacles for tails!'

'Oh calm down,' Steve said, prodding the colourful

seahorse with his nose. It spun just as the octopus had and revealed a multicoloured watery portal.

Beattie pulled him back before he could disappear inside. She didn't want Steve getting lost.

Meanwhile, Maritza was busy transforming the other sea creatures into swirling portals.

'A long time ago, when water witches were every-where and Frostopia ruled the mermaid kingdoms,' Maritza explained, 'this magic wall was built to connect all the realms.'

She touched the final creature – a pink dolphin.

'It's called Realm Reach, and it will take you to any mermaid realm in the world in a single swish of the tail.'

Beattie looked at Paris, whose mouth was hanging open so wide a fish swam inside.

Maritza rushed back to them, her tail flicking fast. 'Frostopia has been largely cut off from the rest of the world for many years.'

'So Realm Reach was forgotten,' Beattie said.

Maritza nodded sadly. 'We seemed more interested in arguing, or ignoring each other completely. I have

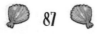

kept watch over the wall in the hope that one day the world would be a better place and mermaids would use it again. Gulper and Rose showed up long after Realm Reach was forgotten, so they don't know it exists.'

Beattie swam up to the Pinkly Lagoon portal, where Gulper and Rose had said they were going. It was dark inside, but Beattie could feel the water was warm and it smelled of sun-soaked sand.

Zelda began swishing her tail excitedly. 'With this wall we can reach the other realms before Gulper and Rose! They don't stand a chance!'

'What's the ice creature in Pinkly Lagoon?' Paris asked.

'A leech,' Maritza Mist said, making Paris tense up. 'Pinkly Lagoon is famous for its leeches.'

Maritza swam over to a block of ice not much taller than herself and raised her hands again. The ice exploded, revealing a battered old vending machine hidden within.

'An axolotl vending machine!' Zelda cried. 'We have one of those in the Hidden Lagoon. It contains small creatures for carrying big things.'

'I invented them!' Maritza Mist said, banging the vending machine with her tail. "They put one here for mermaids going on shopping trips to other realms. They need those axolotls to carry their shopping.'

An axolotl dropped out of the slot and rolled into her hand.

 89

'Hello, dear Grubs, it's been a long time,' she said, stroking the axolotl affectionately. She placed him in Mimi's hand. 'He will help you carry the ice creatures – they can be heavy, even though they're small. He's my most trusty sea-creature friend. He's been living here for thousands of years waiting for mermaids to return to the wall. I tried to get him to move, but he wouldn't.'

Mimi stroked Grubs as he nuzzled into her hand.

'Take care of him,' Maritza said, gazing at him fondly. 'He is very special to me.'

'He says you're very special to him too,' Mimi said.

'Aren't you coming?' Beattie asked.

'No,' Maritza said quietly.

'You'd better have a good reason,' Zelda said, folding her arms crossly. She didn't like anyone who wasn't a team player. It wasn't the shockey way.

'Actually, I have three reasons,' Maritza said. 'Firstly, Gulper and Rose might try to steal more magic from my igloo – that's why they raided the place – so I need to get back and make sure my potions are well protected and hidden.'

'And secondly?' Zelda said, thawing slightly.

'Secondly, I need to find out where that goblin shark was taking Gronnyupple. Can you tell me anything about it?'

'It had amber eyes and was covered in amber jewels,' Beattie said.

'Amberberg then,' Maritza said.

'Pardon?' Beattie, Mimi, Zelda and Paris all said at once.

Maritza pointed to the amber-coloured swirling portal. 'A city where the palaces are carved in amber. Plus they use goblin sharks to collect criminals.'

'Criminals?' Beattie choked.

'Yes, criminals, dear. I can't leave the igloo, but I'll find out as much as I can, so that once we've defeated Gulper and Rose we can *all* go and get Gronnyupple.'

Beattie reluctantly nodded. It seemed mean not to rescue Gronnyupple now that they knew where she was. But they didn't have much choice.

'And thirdly, the Burguin shop in the Glisten Quarter is having a major sale today.'

'Oooh,' Mimi said, looking down at her Burguin T-shirt. 'Can you get me something?'

Maritza Mist winked. 'Remember, head for Vampire Rocks – you'll find the leech in the old part of town, down the darkest alleyway.'

'LET'S DO THIS!' Zelda roared. She and Paris dived excitedly through the portal to Pinkly Lagoon.

'This was meant to be a little detour to check Maritza Mist was OK,' Beattie mumbled to Steve. 'And now we're saving the world.'

'You *hope*,' Steve said.

17

The Glorious Pinkness of Pinkly

Steve floated in silence in Flicko City, the capital of Pinkly Lagoon. If he'd had more of a mouth, his jaw would have been on the floor.

The portal had taken them right to the middle of town, where chattering seahorses whizzed past every few seconds.

'I thought I was the only talking seahorse in the world,' Steve said glumly. 'I'm not a miracle and it's been proven otherwise ... I'm *normal*. THIS IS HORRIFIC!'

Mermaids floated past, unaware that Beattie and the others had just arrived via portal from another realm. Most of them had pink tails – the older the mermaid the more neon-pink the tail.

'Afternoon,' a really ancient mermaid croaked, nearly blinding them.

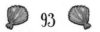

Mimi put on her sunglasses.

Dolphins somersaulted around them, and multicoloured fish weaved in and out of pastel-pink mermaid townhouses nestled in the coral reef.

Paris shook her necklace and morphed into a dolphin.

Beattie spotted a group of cool-looking mermaids floating nearby – one had a pink top with shell sleeves and another had a gold dolphin choker.

Feeling inadequately dressed, Beattie swam down a road called Skerry Street and stopped next to a clump of singing seahorses.

'Excuse me, which way to Vampire Rocks?'

'Leeeeeffffttt,' the seahorses chimed in sync.

And off Beattie and her friends went, towards a highway filled with dolphins pulling mermaids to their destinations.

'I'M NOT A TAXI,' Paris shouted as a group of mermaids grabbed hold of her fin, but it came out as 'Eeeeee ee EE'.

'Steady up!' one of them yelled, shaking Paris and making her morph back into a mermaid.

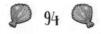

94

The mermaids holding her fin screamed and shot off in all directions. Zelda laughed as they dipped and dived to avoid the traffic.

It wasn't long before the highway trickled out into a glistening pink lagoon. Mermaids leapt out of the shallow water on to lilos that floated on the surface.

Beattie and the others nervously raised their heads out of the water. They were in a human cove, but there wasn't a single human in sight, just thousands of mermaids floating on lilos.

'This is so dangerous,' Beattie said, looking around her. 'Guys … ?'

But they'd gone.

Beattie craned her neck to get a better look and spotted them lazing on the lilos!

Steve bounced back into the water, gasping for breath. 'Too … much … air.'

'Get back here,' Beattie ordered as Zelda leapt on to Mimi's lilo, making her topple over with a splash.

'HUMAN!' someone suddenly roared.

Thousands of mermaids dived back into the water as

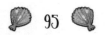

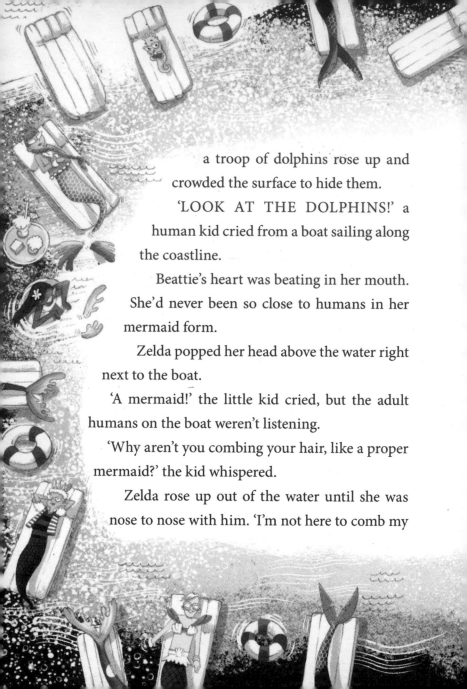

a troop of dolphins rose up and crowded the surface to hide them.

'LOOK AT THE DOLPHINS!' a human kid cried from a boat sailing along the coastline.

Beattie's heart was beating in her mouth. She'd never been so close to humans in her mermaid form.

Zelda popped her head above the water right next to the boat.

'A mermaid!' the little kid cried, but the adult humans on the boat weren't listening.

'Why aren't you combing your hair, like a proper mermaid?' the kid whispered.

Zelda rose up out of the water until she was nose to nose with him. 'I'm not here to comb my

hair. I'm here to *save the world*.'

'Zelda!' Beattie snapped, pulling her back under. 'Stop talking to the human.'

They floated silently under the dolphins until the boat with the humans sailed on.

'BACK TO LAZING AROUND!' a mermaid cried, and they burst out of the water once again.

'And they do this for a *holiday*?' Beattie said, practically hyperventilating.

'Oh come on,' Zelda said, heaving Beattie on to a lilo. 'It's fun!'

Beattie looked over at Mimi, who was applying sun cream to Paris's face.

'We don't have time for this,' Beattie groaned. 'And where's Grubs?'

Steve's head popped out of the water. 'I have some bad news.'

18

How Do You Get an Axolotl Out of a Vending Machine, and Other Important Questions

The problem with the axolotl vending machines was that they were very popular – in every mermaid kingdom.

'The mermaid took it,' Steve said, swishing his tail. 'And put it in ...' He prodded the vending machine with his nose.

'How do we know which one is ours?' Beattie asked. 'Oh, it could take all day for it to spit out the right axolotl!'

Mimi put an ear to the vending machine. 'I'll listen for his voice.'

But it was soundproof. She couldn't hear a thing.

 98

Zelda charged and hit it with a *clang*.

'Argh!' she cried, when she didn't even dent it.

Paris scooped some stray Pinkly pounds from the ground and slotted them into the vending machine.

An axolotl fell out.

'No,' Mimi said. 'That one's got a Pinkly accent.'

Paris tried again.

'That one is just RUDE,' Mimi said.

Paris slotted in the last coin.

A fat fish flopped out.

'That's a fish,' Mimi said helpfully.

'We could come back for Grubs later?' Zelda suggested. 'He's used to being inside vending machines!'

'Grubs is Maritza's special axolotl!' Beattie cried. 'We can't leave him — what if another mermaid gets him and he's lost forever? Oh WHY DOES THIS STUFF ALWAYS HAPPEN TO ME?!'

'This has never happened to you before,' Zelda said. 'You've never had an axolotl called Grubs who got stuck in a vending machine.'

'I meant STUFF *LIKE* THIS!' Beattie clarified.

A queue of mermaids began to form behind them, all eager to use the vending machine.

'There's only one solution, but it will involve swimming very fast afterwards,' Zelda said, moving towards Paris.

'What?' Beattie asked nervously.

Zelda whispered in Paris's ear, then grabbed her necklace and shook it. With a *snap*, she morphed into a huge shark, took a bite out of the top of the vending machine, and axolotls spewed out everywhere!

'Grubs!' Mimi cried, scooping up a small axolotl.

'FREE AXOLOTLS!' the mermaids in the queue cried, grabbing fistfuls of them and kissing their little faces.

A siren sounded. Mermaids with dolphin tails and dolphin-shaped sunglasses appeared. 'STOP RIGHT THERE, BAD MERMAIDS!'

'This is the swimming fast bit,' Zelda said, grabbing Beattie's arm and pulling her through the winding coral paths towards a sign that read *VAMPIRE ROCKS*.

19

Meri and the Burguin Sale

Meri smiled as she detached her clam car from the roof of the bus and climbed into the driver's seat. 'I hope we meet again one day, Jelly!' she shouted out of the window.

'I ONLY MEET MERMAIDS IN TROUBLE, SO I HOPE NOT!' Jelly shouted back, and with a honk of Quentin the jellyfish's horn the whale bus took off.

'Right,' Meri said, punching the controls and steering the clam car towards Frostopia's ice wall. There was a whirring sound, and in one swift twist the clam car burrowed into the ice.

Meri checked the controls. 'Lady Wriggles, do you know where we will emerge once we get to the other side of the wall?'

Lady Wriggles consulted the screens and punched some buttons.

BURGUIN SALE popped up.

'What's … Burguin sale?' Meri whispered.

After about five minutes, Meri and Lady Wriggles found themselves in the midst of what looked like a riot.

'I WANT PARTY-EDITION BURGUIN!'

'GIVE ME THAT GREEN HAMBURGER! I NEED GREEN TO COMPLETE THE SET!'

'WILL YOU STOP SLAPPING LIMITED-EDITION GOLD BURGUIN IN THE FACE! HIS BEAK IS *FRAGILE!*'

'Excuse me,' Meri said quietly to a mermaid wearing a stack of caps with a sort of burger-penguin cartoon on them. 'Are you at war?'

'WE'RE SALE SHOPPING!' the mermaid roared, grabbing a tiny multicoloured burger and flipping it open. A little model of the burger-penguin floated out.

'OH, YOU GOT BIKINI BURGUIN!' a mermaid

shouted as she floated past. 'THAT'S SO UNFAIR! I'VE BEEN TRYING TO FIND THAT ONE FOR YEARS!'

Meri grabbed a burger. 'Burguin,' she said, reading the label, 'is half burger, half penguin. The most popular cartoon character in Frostopia. Find the ice Burguin and you get an eternal supply of Burguin merchandise and a chance to visit the Burguin Studios in Floe.'

Meri tossed the burger over her shoulder. 'So it's not a war,' she said to Lady Wriggles, 'it's *shopping*. They

 103

seem almost the same thing—' Meri stopped. Across the frozen room of hysterical mermaids was a young-looking mermaid with three icy buns on her head.

'Maritza Mist!' she shouted, before realising how not-at-all stealth she was being.

The mermaid with the three buns spun round in shock.

'You made me drop my Burguin burgers,' Maritza Mist said.

Meri straightened her tail and floated perfectly upright.

'Please confirm the status of your health,' she said robotically.

'Still immortal,' Maritza Mist said, trying not to smile. 'You must be from Fortress Bay.'

'And,' Meri coughed, 'please advise the status of the ice narwhal, if known.'

'On its way to Pinkly Lagoon,' Maritza Mist said.

'PINKLY?!' Meri roared, making all the mermaids drop their Burguins. 'Well then, I have to go there too.'

'I know a shortcut,' Maritza Mist said.

THE FREEZY

Frostopia's Coolest Magazine!

BURGUIN INTERVIEW!

Today we interviewed Izzy Iceberger of Flurry Falls, who has found the very rare Bikini Burguin! Bikini Burguin is like Original Burguin, but he's wearing a bikini.

Reporter: Izzy, how did you find Bikini Burguin?

Izzy: I bought him in a shop.

Reporter: That must've been expensive, Bikini Burguin is very rare.

Izzy: Yes, I sold my house.

Reporter: Doesn't your house belong to your parents?

Izzy: Yes, but now it also belongs to Mrs Melterson, who bought it in exchange for the money I needed to buy Bikini Burguin.

Reporter: Aren't your parents ... angry?

Izzy: They don't know yet.

Reporter: But Mrs Melterson will be in your house, with all her stuff. What if she redecorates the place — how will you explain that to your parents?

Izzy: I'll tell them Mrs Melterson is an interior designer who gave the house a makeover.

Reporter: And what if Mrs Melterson eats food from the fridge?

Izzy: I'll say she's a robber.

Reporter: Thank you, Izzy Iceberger!

20

Vampire Rocks and the Ice Leech

Vampire Rocks stretched out in front of Beattie – a lumpy expanse covered in mermaids covered in leeches.

'Welcome to Vampire Rocks Leech Spa. How many, please?'

'NONE,' Zelda said, disgusted.

Beattie nudged her with her tail. 'Zelda, the ice creature is in there.'

'Yeah,' Zelda said. 'But Maritza failed to tell us the old part of town is now a LEECH SPA.'

'We're not here for the spa,' Paris said. 'We just want to swim around.'

'That's nice,' the mermaid said, sounding like she didn't think it was nice at all. 'But no one's allowed past me without a spa ticket.'

'Four and a seahorse, then,' Zelda said reluctantly.

A shower of leeches rained down on them.

'MERS MON IN MY MOUF!' Beattie cried, spitting in disgust.

'Spa rules! You must stay still when in the spa and remain in your allocated spa bed. We hope you have a relaxing experience,' the mermaid oozed. 'Would anyone like a glass of Gloopy?'

Moving, let alone swimming, was nearly impossible in the leech spa – they were covered from head to tail in leeches, and the glasses of Gloopy made them sleepy.

Beattie's tail felt heavy and there was a leech sucking on her eyebrow. A clock floated in front of her, with a little rainbowfish moving the hands.

'YOU'LL BE GORGEOUS AT HALF PAST THE RAINBOWFISH!' the mermaid in charge of the spa shouted as she swam past.

'I'll be gorgeous when we get the ice leech,' Zelda said. 'Gorgeously happy anyway.'

Mimi peeled the leeches off her face and rolled on to her belly. 'The rainbowfish says the old town streets run under the spa. We can reach them from those caves over there behind the rocks.'

'Let's go before the owner comes back,' Zelda hissed, swimming fast towards the rocks. Mimi followed her.

'Beattie,' Paris whispered. 'Where's Steve?'

Beattie looked around. She could only see mermaids covered in leeches and clocks with rainbowfish.

'YOU'LL BE GORGEOUS AT HALF PAST THE RAINBOWFISH!'

'Steve?' Beattie said, scanning the water for him.

'He'll be fine,' Zelda whispered. 'We'll be back in no time. Now, come on!'

They dived into a crack in the rocks, slithering down until they hit sand and the rocks opened into a tunnel.

Beattie had a horrible feeling, and it wasn't because the leech was still on her eyebrow.

21

Long-Lost Steve

Steve floated in the seahorse section of the Vampire Rocks spa. It was different from the mermaid section, with bubbling baths of leech juice for them to stew in, and tiny cocktails of Gloopy.

Steve had gone a bit cross-eyed from drinking too much of it.

'You visiting for long?' the seahorse bubbling next to him asked.

'No, just a quick holiday,' Steve lied. 'Do you live here?'

'Live here?' the seahorse laughed. 'Seahorses don't *live* here, silly! Have you been drinking that Gloopy through your nose?! We're *all* from Rainbow Landing – we just holiday here, like you. My name's Stella.'

'Steve,' he replied.

She gasped and slipped under the leech juice. He

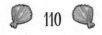 110

knew he was an impressive seahorse, even if he was no longer a miracle, but he'd never got that kind of reaction for just saying his name.

'Hello?' Steve called.

The leech juice bubbled.

Stella burst back up, coughing and spluttering. 'You're Steve?'

'Yes,' Steve replied.

'Long-lost Steve!'

'Well, actually I usually go by Steve and at the very

 111

most *Miracle*, because where I live I'm the only talking seahorse.'

'So you're *not* from Rainbow Landing. You *are* Long-lost Steve!'

'I'm pretty sure I'm just Steve,' Steve said. 'I was found next to a sunken ship, yelling at some tuna. The mermaid who found me gave me to her daughter as a pet of sorts, and I've been part of their family ever since. Most would argue the best part of their family. And by most, I mean me.'

'YOU ARE LONG-LOST STEVE! ARROGANT LONG-LOST STEVE!' Stella cried. 'EVERYONE!' she yelled across to the thousands of other seahorses stewing in leech-juice pools. 'IT'S LONG-LOST STEVE!'

A ripple of excitement spread through the spa.

'Who is Long-lost Steve?' Steve whispered.

'He's the missing seahorse. The son of rock stars Stevie and Steven!'

'Rock stars?' Steve said, his eyes lighting up.

Stella nodded. 'I'm heading back to Rainbow

Landing today – come with me! I can reunite you.'

'But … my family. My Beattie, she would never –'
Steve looked over the rocks and down to the level below,
where Beattie had been lying covered in leeches –
'leave me,' he finished in surprise when he realised she
was *gone*.

22

Nightmare Dolphin

'So this was the Pinkly Lagoon of the olden days,' Beattie said as they passed ancient caves with seaweed-lined windows. There were no Burguin cartoons, swimways or clam cars.

Mimi, who had swum ahead, was charging back towards them in a burst of speed.

'The good news is, I've found the ice leech,' she said.

'YES!' Beattie roared, swimming faster.

'The bad news is that a dolphin is swimming away with it.'

The ground began to rumble and the rock walls started to crumble as two pink dolphins came into view.

'Eeee E eeeee EeeeEEEEeee,' the bigger dolphin squeaked.

'It's telling the other dolphin that she should've only

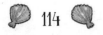 114

drunk one of the potions, like the label said,' Mimi translated for the others.

'Potions? Wait a minute!' Beattie cried. 'They're not dolphins, they're Gulper and Rose in disguise!'

Rose was growing bigger and bigger – she could barely fit in the cramped tunnel – and at the same time her face was becoming more and more mermaid-like. It wasn't long before she looked like a dolphin with a mermaid nose and eyebrows.

'IT'S LIKE A NIGHTMARE!' Zelda screamed, trying to squeeze past.

'SHE'S GOING TO BURST!' Paris cried, just as the rock walls gave way, releasing Rose the gigantic dolphin on to the unsuspecting spa mermaids above. Beattie shielded her face as rocks and leeches rained down on her like the worst shower in the world.

'GIANT DOLPHIN ATTACK!' a mermaid screeched overhead. They swam in all directions, smacking into each other and shrieking.

Rose and Gulper shot off.

'Cods,' Beattie said as she sat down on a rock next to

Zelda and surveyed the scene. Leeches went flying past their noses as mermaids flopped about in the wreckage.

'And this,' Zelda said, gesticulating with a leech, 'is why you'll never find me at a spa.'

'We were too late,' Beattie grumbled as they swam back towards the spa reception.

'Well, technically it wasn't our fault,' Zelda pointed out. 'How were we supposed to know someone would scoop up Grubs and put him in a vending machine?'

'If you hadn't been playing on the lilos, it would never have happened,' Beattie said, crossing her arms angrily.

'But you said you LOVED the lilos!' Zelda said.

'No I didn't,' Beattie protested.

'Oh yeah, that was Steve. Never mind.'

'Steve!' Beattie said, looking around. 'We have to get him before we go.'

'We hope you enjoyed your leechy, beachy spa experience,' the spa mermaid said, her hair pasted to

her face and a leech up each nostril. 'We're sorry the spa collapsed and a nightmare dolphin tried to kill us all. To apologise for this inconvenience, your spa treatment today is free. We hope to see you soon, so you can become gorgeous at half past the rainbowfish!'

'We've got to pick up Steve, our seahorse,' Beattie said. 'He's still inside somewhere.'

'Oh, Steve,' the mermaid said. 'He left.'

'Left?' Beattie said.

'Jumped on the dolphin balloon to Rainbow Landing, just before the place crumbled.'

'Dolphin balloon?' Beattie said in disbelief.

'It's like a hot-air balloon,' the mermaid said flatly. 'We stole the idea from the humans. It's attached to a dolphin, then the basket is filled with seahorses, and the dolphin swims to Rainbow Landing, diving every so often so the seahorses can be dunked in water to breathe.'

'Does it travel fast?' Beattie asked.

'Oh yes,' the mermaid said. 'He's well on his way to Rainbow Landing.'

THE FREEZY
Frostopia's Coolest Magazine!

BURGUIN INTERVIEW!

Today we interviewed Aimi McWhale of Floe, who has found an Original Burguin! Original Burguin looks like Original Burguin, because they are the same thing and almost everyone in Frostopia has one.

Reporter: Aimi, you have an Original Burguin.
Aimi: Is it a rare one?
Reporter: No.
Aimi: I need to find a rare one then. Maybe I'll get my pet seal on the job. She's called Slippy and she likes to slime mermaids.
Reporter: Is that why I'm covered in slime?
Aimi: Maaaaayyyybeeee.
Reporter: Thank you, Aimi McWhale!

23

Meri Makes Some Friends

Beattie dived through the portal to Realm Reach in shocked silence. Steve was gone.

'Well, they may have the ice leech, but we have Realm Reach!' Zelda said, trying to cheer everyone up.

'And now so do we,' came a whisper as Gulper and Rose squeezed through the portal. 'Thanks for the tip. This will be much quicker than swimming – even with speedy potions, it still takes a *loooong* time!'

They disappeared through the portal to Octopolli.

'Did that just happen?' Zelda said, rubbing her eyes. 'Did Gulper and Rose just follow us here?'

'They've gone to Octopolli!' Beattie cried. 'Ugh, we're so *bad* at this!'

'So we'll go somewhere else,' Paris said. 'Let them get the ice creature in Octopolli. We'll go to—'

'The Kingdom of Mume,' Zelda finished.

'No,' Beattie said firmly. 'We need to follow them. You saw what havoc they caused at the spa – they might *hurt* someone in Octopolli.'

'But, Beattie,' Zelda protested, 'we only need one ice creature to stop them – what's the point in chasing them?'

Beattie thought for a moment. She pictured all the mermaids lazing at the leech spa fleeing in a leech-smeared panic. 'No. We know where they're going, so we have a responsibility to protect other mermaids.'

'Fine,' Zelda said. 'But for the record, my idea is better.'

Grubs began wriggling as Maritza Mist floated around the corner. She stopped when she saw their faces. 'No luck, dears?'

Beattie looked down at her tail. Maritza had trusted them and they'd messed it up.

'Well, I have someone to help you,' Maritza said as a mermaid with jet-black hair and a determined smile appeared beside her.

'I'm Meri,' she said shyly. 'I've been *waaaaatching* you.'

'Tone it down,' Maritza said. 'That sounded creepy.'

'Ah,' Mimi said. 'Merry! Just like all the sea creatures in Frostopia. What's your name?'

Meri paused. 'No, um, my name is Meri. With an i.'

Mimi looked confused.

'She's from Fortress Bay, the spy school in the Arabian Sea,' Maritza explained.

Meri shifted awkwardly. 'I'm, um, sort of meant to be undercover.'

'She's undercover, dears.'

'I'm here to help,' Meri said as Maritza nudged her forward. 'I know the locations of the ice creatures. It was my job to protect the list and the ice narwhal. I know that list off by heart!'

'ISN'T THAT JUST WHAT WE NEEDED?!' Maritza said cheerily. 'I'd forgotten where I'd hidden most of them, so you have helped hugely already. YOU'RE THE BEST SPY MERMAID IN THE WORLD, DEAR!'

'I'm actually pretty average,' Meri mumbled.

 121

'She has a jellyfish in her hair,' Paris whispered to Zelda.

'I also have news of Gronnyupple,' Maritza said. 'Meri and I have established that she is alive and well in Amberberg, where they think she's a criminal mastermind.'

'But she's not a criminal mastermind!' Zelda scoffed. 'Wait … Maybe she was just pretending to be goofy and weird!'

'She's completely innocent,' Meri said. 'It looks like she's been framed, but I don't know why. Maritza is going to look into it while we go after Gulper and Rose. She'll try to break her out, but it won't be easy. Amberberg has the toughest goblin sharks in the world.'

'But who would frame Gronnyupple?' Beattie asked. 'Who even knows Gronnyupple? She's a loner. She lives in the Crocodile Kingdom and hangs out in an abandoned launderette, where she practises spells.'

'It's very strange,' Meri said. 'I wonder if Gulper and Rose could've had a hand in it.'

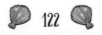

'But why Gronnyupple?' Paris asked. 'She wouldn't hurt a fish. She's hardly a threat to them.'

'It might be part of a bigger plan,' Meri said. 'It's too soon to tell. But the fact that she's a water witch might be significant. Now, let's get on with the mission.'

'Steve would love to meet a spy,' Beattie said quietly as she stared at the empty false teeth.

'I've been following your progress so far,' Meri said, pointing at her tail. 'Spy mermaids can see anywhere in the world on their tails.'

'Did you see where Steve went?' Beattie asked hopefully.

Meri looked at her blankly. 'Who?'

Beattie sighed. 'Never mind.' She looked up at the multicoloured Rainbow Landing portal. Her chances of getting there, locating Steve and getting back before Gulper and Rose found the ice creature in Octopolli seemed small.

'Beattie,' Zelda said, nudging her.

'I don't understand why he would leave me,' Beattie said as her eyes welled with tears.

Mimi sidled up beside her. 'It might be an insensitive moment to mention it, but this rainbowfish is wondering if Steve's false teeth bedroom is available to rent? He'd very much like to live in them.'

Beattie snapped the false teeth closed and dived through the portal to Octopolli.

'We'll find him, Beattie!' Zelda cried as she raced after her.

'After we get the ice creature from Octopolli!' Paris added as she dived through.

Mimi stared at the rainbowfish. 'I'm afraid it's a firm no on the rental.'

24

Slippery Octopolli

The Realm Reach portal took them to Inko, the biggest city in Octopolli.

It was dark, with murky grey water and ink-black buildings. Mermaids with octopus tentacles slunk past suspiciously.

'Would you rather have an octopus tail that constantly picked your nose, or an octopus head?' Zelda asked.

Mimi and Paris seriously considered the question.

'Would the tentacles hurt when picking my nose?' Mimi asked.

Paris tapped her chin. 'Would I be allowed to wear earrings if I had an octopus head?'

'I'm so sorry about them,' Beattie whispered to Meri.

'It's not a problem,' Meri said. 'I share a room with

the Teenies – triplet mermaids – at spy school and they're far worse. This is actually fun!'

Beattie wondered what it was like at Fortress Bay, and what spy school involved.

'The ice octopus is hidden in the Beak de Beak area of Octopolli,' Meri went on.

'Perfect – let's figure out how to get there,' Beattie said as Zelda and Paris helped Mimi put an octopus tentacle up her nose.

'It does hurt!'

THE FREEZY
Frostopia's Coolest Magazine!

BURGUIN INTERVIEW!

Today we interviewed Ralph Snowland of the Glisten Quarter, who has found the Seahorse Surprise Burguin! Seahorse Surprise Burguin looks like Original Burguin, but he's hiding Seahorse Surprise sweets in his burger bun!

Reporter: Ralph, what did you do when you found Seahorse Surprise Burguin?

Ralph: I screamed!

Reporter: Because you were so delighted, I'm sure!

Ralph: I had just found out that Gillica, who plays Blubble the Ice-Skating Seal, was CANCELLING her shows because some other mermaids pretended to be her and then ran away, so she wasn't allowed into Frostopia and went home – and that is why I screamed.

Reporter: Weren't you happy to find the Seahorse Surprise Burguin though? They are pretty rare!

Ralph: I don't really know what Burguin is. I screamed my way into the Burguin shop and got it by accident.

Reporter: How is that even possible?

Ralph: They threw it at me to get me to stop screaming, but it landed in my mouth so I got to keep it.

Reporter: Thank you, Ralph!

25

Beak de Beak

A long cage weaved around Inko city like a sinister caterpillar. Inside, Beattie could see mermaids riding huge gold tentacles, slithering fast to their destinations.

'The Inko Express will take us to Beak de Beak,' Meri said, pointing at the cage. Mermaids were lining up in their hundreds along its edges. 'Inko Express is its official name, but the mermaids of Octopolli call it the Inko Slinko.'

'How come you know so much about other mermaid places?' Zelda asked suspiciously.

'I've studied them all. It's how you become a good spy. For example, I know that in your Hidden Lagoon there's an excellent restaurant called Jawella's inside a shark. I get their chomp chops delivered to the canteen in Fortress Bay by special request.'

'No way!' Zelda said, sounding impressed.

Beattie swam around the Inko Slinko map. Inko was one of seven cities in Octopolli, and Beak de Beak was at the end of the line.

'Is this thing safe?' Paris asked, just before a tentacle carriage slammed against the cage. 'Never mind,' she whimpered.

They waited for an empty one before they opened the cage door and dived on. Beattie tried to get a grip but it was almost impossible, the whole thing was as slippery as – well – an octopus.

They slithered off at breakneck speed.

'IT JUST SEEMS TO BE GOING IN CIRCLES AROUND INKO!' Beattie shouted to Meri, who was balancing side-saddle on the tentacle carriage with ease.

'Beattie, *look*!' Paris yelled as the seabed beneath them opened up to reveal a pit of glowing jellyfish.

'OH COD!' Beattie cried, grabbing on to Paris and Mimi just as the carriage plunged into the pit.

'I HAVE A JELLYFISH STUCK TO MY FAAAACCEEEE!' Zelda roared, peeling it off, just as another one attached itself to her hair.

They hurtled through a dark passageway, where eels popped out of caves holding little seaweed flyers.

VISIT THE POD BOX IN PODLEY, the best gallery for sunken human paintings! We have a new drawing by the incredibly popular human artist Teddyage4. Plus some fascinating doodles by Homework.

The Inko Slinko whipped on through another clump of jellyfish, only this time they extended their stingers as the carriage passed through.

'The stingers are slowing us down,' Beattie said in amazement as they reached a caged area.

'SLIPPERY ROCK,' came a crackle. 'PLEASE SLINK OFF HERE FOR SLIPPERY ROCK.'

Zelda pointed enthusiastically at a poster. 'Look, Beatts! Slippery Rock is home to the best swimming complex in Octopolli, with over a thousand whirlpools and a never-ending flume. I want to go on the never-ending flume!'

'Read the rest,' Beattie said. 'It says only one mermaid has ever got on the never-ending flume, and she's still on it, *ninety-five* years later.'

'What a way to spend ninety-five years,' Zelda said dreamily.

They shot off again, passing Squiddy Circus, home to a circus run by a squid, then around a bend full of the largest sunken ships Beattie had ever seen, before stopping to refuel at Ringsworth, the location of the

world's only finishing school for octopuses.

Beattie was getting impatient.

'Look!' Paris shouted. 'UP AHEAD! It's Gulper and Rose!'

'Where?' Meri said, staring at her tail, trying to get a better view.

'About nine carriages ahead,' Paris said as she tried to flop off the tentacle carriage. Its tip smacked her, pushing her back on.

Meri tapped her tail. 'Good spot. They'll reach Beak de Beak five minutes before us. We have to slow them down.'

'How?' Beattie said, just as Mimi fell forward, clutching her ears. Meri did the same.

Zelda grabbed her twin's shoulders and shook them. 'Mimi! What is it?'

'MERI PEBBLE! MERI PEBBLE! MERI PEBBLE!' boomed all the passing eels and octopuses.

'MERI,' Mimi said loudly. 'SOMEONE'S CALLING YOU.'

'Oh no,' Meri said, curling into a ball. 'It's Sabrina.

She's discovered I left Fortress Bay. I really thought that whale I dressed up in my clothes would've fooled her ...'

'MERI PEBBLE! RETURN TO BASE AT ONCE!'

'LOOK AHEAD ON THE TENTACLE CARRIAGES!' Meri shouted to Sabrina. 'THE VIPERVIEW PRISON ESCAPEES ARE RIDING THE INKO SLINKO!'

'MERI,' an eel said sternly, while Mimi translated for the non-fishtalkers. 'THIS IS BEYOND RIDICULOUS NOW. YOU STOLE THE MOST EXPENSIVE CLAM CAR TOO.'

Lady Wriggles burrowed deeper into Meri's hair.

'I CAN SEE YOU, LADY WRIGGLES!' Sabrina's voice boomed.

'I'll be back soon!' Meri said, defiantly pushing the eel away.

'You left Fortress Bay without permission?' Zelda said.

'Sabrina didn't believe me about Gulper and Rose,' Meri said. 'She showed me footage of them in

Viperview – they look exactly the same, but they can't be in two places at once.'

'Wait,' Beattie said. 'Did either of them say FISH EYE?'

'Yes,' Meri said, sounding shocked. 'How do you know that?'

'Beattie once used one of Maritza Mist's spells on us,' Zelda explained. 'It's a potion that doubles you, but a side effect is your double sometimes shouts FISH EYE!'

'So they used a doubling potion!' Meri said, scrunching up her fist. 'Those cunning mermaids.'

'MERI!' Sabrina yelled. 'IS THIS THING ON? ARE THE SEA CREATURES SHOUTING MY MESSAGES? HELLO?!'

Mimi clutched her ears as the sound increased. She needed to tell Sabrina about the potion!

'MERI!' came Sabrina's roar. But this time it was too loud for all the sea creatures that could hear it. The eels reared up and began to scatter, the octopuses formed what Beattie could only describe as a wriggling panic, and the tentacle carriages began to jump and dive as if they'd forgotten where they were going.

'This is our chance,' Zelda said, grabbing Beattie's arm and pulling her off the tentacle. They swam as fast as they could towards Gulper and Rose. 'It's like I always say, a little chaos can save the day.'

26

Maritza Sends a Shark

Maritza Mist uncorked another bottle of SEAL POP and peered out of the icy window of her igloo. Gulper and Rose were nowhere to be seen, but she'd hidden the potions under her Burguin collection, just to be safe.

'Now,' she said, flipping open the clamshell compact Meri had left for her, 'let's see if we can save Gronnyupple.' She prodded the compact with her finger until a menu came up.

```
SABRINA'S PORTAL
MERMAID SEARCH
SPY CASE DATABASE
REALM ASSISTANCE
```

Maritza pressed Realm Assistance and another menu popped up. She sighed – she wasn't a fan of technology.

```
JELLY PICK-UP
UNDERCOVER MERMAIDS ON LAND
WHALE DIVERSIONS
FISHTALKER TALK
SHARK FRIENDS
```

'Hmm,' she mumbled, before randomly prodding the screen.

Another menu popped up, this time with a selection of Shark Friends photos.

Maritza groaned and clicked the first one.

```
JAWELLA'S SHARK, LOCATED IN THE HAMMERHEAD
HEIGHTS REGION OF THE HIDDEN LAGOON, CURRENTLY
A POPULAR RESTAURANT.
VARIETY: MEGALODON.
SPEED: FAST.
BITE SCOPE: IMPRESSIVE.
MOOD: JOYFUL.
SPECIAL TALENTS: IS ALSO A RESTAURANT.
```

'Perfect,' Maritza said, clicking on it. A live picture flashed up of the Jawella's shark swimming slowly

between the tall rock towers of Hammerhead Heights. It was covered in fairy lights and had a sign that flashed *JAWELLA'S*. Maritza smiled and pressed the 'CALL SHARK' button.

'Rescued by a restaurant,' she said with a nod. 'Gronnyupple will love that.'

27

The Right Ticket

'CARNIVAL!' mermaids roared as they swam up and over the grand rubbery gates.

Clouds of ink wafted past like mist on a spooky day as the bright lights of the Beak de Beak carnival danced across the murky waters.

'TICKETS!' came a shout through the deafening sound of drumming octopuses. Up ahead, Beattie could see a mermaid in a huge headdress supervising a line of jellyfish stamping tickets. And at the very front, holding out a ticket smugly, was Rose Rockweed.

'Unbelievable,' Beattie said.

'You can use your magic to make us some tickets,' Mimi said to her. Then she turned to Meri. 'Beattie is a water witch, but a special one like Maritza – they can make magic.'

'Wow, that's incredibly cool, Beattie,' Meri said. 'We need to get inside and fast. Can you do it?'

They floated in front of Beattie, staring. She wished Steve was here – he would explain how rubbish she was at magic.

'You can do it,' Paris said kindly.

Beattie squeezed her eyes shut and imagined some tickets for the Beak de Beak carnival. She held her hand out and …

'Beatts, these are tickets to a Best Beak contest,' Zelda said, inspecting them. 'In Rainbow Landing.'

'Sorry,' Beattie said. 'I was thinking about Steve. I'll try again.'

She felt the soft squidginess of seaweed in her hand.

'Nope,' Meri said. 'These tickets are for a clam-car and beak-cleaning service in Podley.'

'FISHELBOWS!' Beattie yelled (it was a very rude word).

'Wait, I have an idea,' Paris said, plucking the useless tickets from Beattie's grasp and handing them one each. 'Make sure you let me stamp them.' She shook

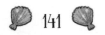

her necklace and morphed into a jellyfish.

'GET BACK TO WORK!' the mermaid with the huge headdress roared at her.

They all wiggled with excitement as Paris the jellyfish wafted off towards the ticket line.

As they got close to the front Beattie could hear her heart pounding in her chest – or perhaps it was the octopus drummers.

Paris took one look at their tickets and zapped them with her stinger.

'Genius,' Beattie whispered as they swam in.

'Now what?' Zelda said, resisting the urge to jump on one of the rides.

Meri pointed at an ornate carousel. It had all sorts of sea creatures whirling around at speed as mermaids cackled and cheered and practically fell off it.

'The ice creature is in the carousel,' Meri said with an awkward cough. 'In the golden dolphin specifically.'

'Great,' Zelda said. 'We'll break it open.'

'The carousel's golden dolphin seat always has a rider on it – it's what mermaids come to this carnival for. Dolphins don't swim in these waters, so none of them have seen one. That's why it's the most popular thing in the whole place!'

'Why didn't Maritza just hide them at the back of her wardrobe or in a trusty fish, like a normal mermaid?' Beattie said as Paris the jellyfish joined them.

'BACK TO WORK!' a mermaid cried, grabbing Paris the jellyfish and flinging her into an arcade stall.

'THROW THE SHELL HAT ON THE JELLYFISH AND WIN BOTH THE SHELL AND THE JELLYFISH!' the mermaid at the stall shouted.

A mesmerised kid mermaid chucked a giant shell, which landed squarely on Paris's jellyfish head.

'Right,' Beattie said, 'everyone remain calm. Zelda, go and get Paris back. Mimi, Meri and I will get the ice creature.'

'*Mimi, Meri and IIIII,*' Mimi sang unhelpfully.

They waded through the forest of tentacles as the crowds of mermaids grew thicker and thicker.

Beattie got as close to the carousel as she could. The golden dolphin seat sailed past her eyeline, taunting her.

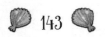

'Mimi,' she said firmly. 'Fin-fu it.'

'But I'm only supposed to use fin-fu for good.'

'THIS *IS* FOR GOOD!' Beattie said.

'But I'll be destroying a special carousel,' Mimi said, clearly in turmoil.

'They can fix it quickly,' Meri said encouragingly. 'Have you seen how many tentacles the mermaids have around here?! It'll take them no time at all!'

Mimi slowly closed her eyes and flicked her finger. The beautiful golden dolphin seat crumbled, pinging the mermaid riding it all the way out of the Beak de Beak carnival.

'He'll be *fine*,' Beattie said. She looked into the crowds, wondering where Gulper and Rose were.

'Beattie,' Meri said, 'the ice creature … it's—'

Beattie scrunched up her fists, expecting the news to be bad.

'HERE!' Meri cried.

Beattie stared into the crumpled seat – curled up in the middle was a tiny ice octopus.

145

Mermaids began to crowd around, whispering.

'NOTHING TO SEE HERE!' Beattie called out. 'JUST A STANDARD MALFUNCTION. VERY TYPICAL OF DOLPHIN-SHAPED THINGS. IT'LL BE FIXED SOON.'

Grubs leapt from Mimi's shoulder and wriggled under the ice creature until it was on his back.

'Did we just do what I think we did?!' Beattie said, spotting Gulper and Rose, who were still waiting to get on the ride.

'WE DID IT!' Meri roared. She composed herself quickly. If spy school had taught her anything it was that if you celebrate a successful mission, the bad guys will take that moment to swoop in and …

'LEAVE US ALONE!' Beattie cried as Gulper and Rose appeared above them.

Mimi fin-fu chopped them and sent them flying into the carousel.

Beattie felt a strange tingling in her tail as all around them the water began to bubble.

'Ooh, the water witch is getting angry,' Gulper

laughed. 'Look at her hair!'

'It's turned red,' Mimi said with a smile.

'What?' Beattie looked around for a mirror.

'And now it's going a bit yellow,' Meri said.

'Oh, it's just hair,' Beattie said. She raised Grubs in the air. 'Who cares when we have Grubs and the ice—'

'*She skates, she glides, she moves from side to side. She's big and she's trouble*,' a voice sang.

A seal lolloped past and knocked Grubs out of Beattie's hand.

'*Yeah ... she's Blubble.*'

Beattie stared in disbelief as Grubs landed in Rose Rockweed's hand. She ripped the ice creature off the poor axolotl and threw him back to Beattie.

'HOW DID THAT SEAL GET IN HERE?!' Beattie roared. 'This is all Zelda's fault for pretending to be Gillica in the first place!'

'Got her!' Zelda said cheerily as she emerged from the crowd with Paris the jellyfish firmly in her grasp. 'Wait – what did I miss?'

28

Paris Rants and Raves about Gulper and Rose

JELLYFISH SILENCE

29

Steve and the Dolphin Balloon

The rainbow-patterned dolphin balloon glided through the air off the south coast of Australia.

The hot sun was beating down on it, casting a rainbow glow across the water.

Steve had been vomiting the whole way there.

The dolphin made to dive again and …

BLEURGH!

They hit the water. When the balloon and basket rose back up into the air, fifty-seven seahorses were covered from head to tail in vomit – and SCREAMING.

'STOP TIMING IT SO YOU THROW UP RIGHT BEFORE WE GO UNDER!' Stella the seahorse shouted at Steve.

The dolphin began to dive again.

'NO! STEVE … DON'T!'

BLEURGH!

'*HOW* MUCH LONGER?' one of the
seahorses wailed.

The dolphin dived again.

BLEURGH!

Steve wiped his nose on the edge of the
basket and slumped over, exhausted.
That's when he saw it, just up ahead –
island upon island covered in rainbow
flags.

And suddenly he felt much better.

30

Jawella's to the Rescue (Sort of)

The Amberberg mermaids heard the Jawella's shark before they saw it.

'Do you hear that swishing? And clinking?'

Mermaids drinking foam shakes in delicate amber teacups stopped and looked around.

'It sounds like plates rattling around in …'

'A SHARK!'

The Jawella's shark came speeding into view and lurched forward, mouth open and –

Ping

– bounced delicately off the building it had been instructed to free Gronnyupple from. It floated on the spot, mouth wide and awaiting further instructions.

'Oooh,' the Amberberg mermaids said, swimming inside the shark's mouth and sitting down for lunch.

'This is nice,' one of them said, picking up a menu. 'What are chomp chops?'

Back in Frostopia, Maritza Mist emerged from her ice mist shower with an icicle towel wrapped around her head. She stared into the clamshell compact and frowned. 'The shark didn't complete its mission? Now, how did that happen?'

She closed the compact. She'd have to think of something else.

31

Steve Arrives at Rainbow Landing

The dolphin dived deeper and deeper until the basket of seahorses spied a glistening coral reef, which rearranged itself in a perfect rainbow as they passed. The purple section of it flipped up and the dolphin swam through.

'Welcome!' boomed a cheery voice. 'TO RAINBOW LANDING!'

Steve spun around, taking it all in. Everything sparkled and mermaids with shiny rainbow tails stopped and waved from their colourful gardens as the dolphin balloon glided by.

On a twinkling bridge separating one rainbow-coloured seahorse house from another, an angelfish played the violin.

They pulled into a rocky area full of resting balloon

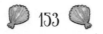

dolphins. A family with eight tiny seahorse babies floated into the basket next to them.

'TO PINKLY FOR HOLIDAY!' the littlest one cheered.

'Steve?' came a voice. 'Long-lost Steve!'

Before Steve knew what was happening, two seahorses were hugging him and crying.

'It's us!' the one that was doing the most crying said. 'It's Stevie and Steven – Mum and Dad! We've found you, after all these years!'

Steve was overwhelmed. It was more of a shock than the time Zelda had convinced him to hug an electric eel. He missed them all a little bit, even Zelda, but he pushed those thoughts aside. After all, they had left him alone in the Vampire Rocks spa.

He was with his real family now.

The seahorses guided Steve in a daze towards a spectacular house covered in candy-cane striped turrets with rainbows beaming from the windows.

'I'm home,' Steve said with a smile. And he meant it.

32

So Many Mermaid Towns, So Little Time

Every time Beattie returned to Realm Reach she liked it less and less.

Maritza greeted them with a big smile. 'Any luck, dears?'

Beattie stared down at her tail.

'We got it,' Meri said. 'But then we lost it.'

'Well, I have news on Gronnyupple,' Maritza said.

Beattie looked up excitedly. 'She's back?'

'No,' Maritza said, still smiling. 'I sent a shark to rescue her, but it didn't work like it was supposed to.'

Meri took the clamshell compact and reviewed the footage. 'It pinged off the building? A megalodon shark? And then it just floated there, being a *restaurant*?'

Maritza nodded.

Meri looked worried.

'What is it?' Beattie asked.

'It's just … strange,' Meri said. 'The shark didn't complete its mission – it was meant to bite into the building so Gronnyupple could swim out and into its mouth. And then she'd be carried home.'

'Maybe the shark wasn't hungry,' Mimi said.

'No,' Meri said quietly. 'It would take some serious magic to stop a spy-mermaid shark attack. And it wasn't Gulper and Rose because they were in Octopolli, not Amberberg. Someone else must've done it … maybe there's a water witch in Amberberg that we don't know about, who is more powerful than we could ever imagine. But that's almost impossible!'

'Well, that's a mystery for another time,' Maritza said. 'Gulper and Rose just dived through the portal to Jewelport – and you're running out of time.'

The chase was on.

The mermaids headed to Jewelport, a trading town filled with gems and trunks of treasure.

'I'VE GOT GEMS IN MY EYES!' Zelda shouted, as Gulper and Rose burst from a pile of jewels with an ice turtle.

Paris tried to whack them with a treasure chest, but it just flattened Rose's face.

'LOO LAN'T LOP US,' she said with a squint smirk as she squashed her face back together.

'I don't think I can swim much further,' Beattie wheezed.

'Come on, Beattie!' Zelda roared. 'Back to Realm Reach. Pick up the pace!'

Every time they passed the multicoloured portal to Rainbow Landing, Beattie wanted nothing more than to dive inside and find Steve.

'There's no ice creature in Rainbow Landing, Beattie,' Zelda would remind her. 'Gulper and Rose got that one years ago.'

They tore through the different realms, losing with

ease. They swam fast in the Hidden Lagoon, in case their friends from home spotted them, and chomped their way through Jellywiches and another defeat in the Crocodile Kingdom.

They dived through the Hermit Grove portal and into darkness. It was night-time there, but Gulper and Rose emerged from the gloom with grim smiles pasted on their faces.

Gulper was holding an ice crab.

'Ugh,' Meri said as a family of hermit crabs attached themselves to her ears.

Next was the only portal as icy cold as Frostopia –
Beluga Town!

'WELL, HELLO THERE, FRIENDS. WELCOME
TO BELUGA TOWN!' chirped a mermaid called
Moira Wet. 'The exclamation mark is actually in the
town's name, because we're so excited you're here!'

They'd arrived at the Shrimpol station on the edge
of town. A huge swirl of ice stretched beneath them
as far as the eye could see. Mermaids proceeded
through the swirl, some free-swimming, others on
sledges pulled by beluga whales. Moira Wet, Beluga
Town!'s most loved mermaid, was guiding beluga
whales into bays and sticking Shrimpol pumps in their
mouths.

'Right,' Beattie said, hurrying towards the swirl,
'let's finally get an ice creature!'

Meri stopped in front of a whale so ancient it was
barely moving.

'It's not—' Beattie said quietly.

The whale did an almighty burp and spat out Gulper
and Rose.

'HIDDEN IN THE ANCIENT WHALE!' Rose bellowed, holding up a tiny ice whale.

'OH COME ON!' Beattie cried.

'See you in Amberberg,' Gulper said with a smirk.

Zelda turned to Beattie. 'We're going to Mume – it's time we tried my plan. There are only two ice creatures left – in Amberberg and Mume. This is our last chance to outsmart them.'

THE FREEZY

Frostopia's Coolest Magazine!

BURGUIN INTERVIEW!

Today we interviewed Patricia von Polar of Floe, who has found the rarest Burguin of all – the Ice Burguin! Ice Burguin looks like Original Burguin but is made of ice.

Reporter: Patricia, you found the rarest Burguin of them all – how do you feel?
Patricia: I LOST IT!
Reporter: That's so great – wait, what?
Patricia: It slipped out of my hand when a seal slimed me – almost certainly on purpose!
Reporter: If you could send a message to the seal who did this, what would you say?
Patricia: I don't speak seal.
Reporter: Thank you, Patricia von Polar!

33

Seahorse Life

Steve swam down Rainbow Landing's main street, with its multicoloured shops and fabulously dressed mermaids. He bought a tiny Sparkle Shake in a colourful cup and a rainbow-patterned cone top. And he paid for them in smiles.

'Look!' seahorses cried as he passed. 'It's Long-lost Steve!'

His parents zoomed by, wearing their fancy shell jetpacks, which made them go extremely fast. 'Don't be home too late,' they called. 'We're having a party for you!'

He picked up a copy of *Seahorse Sunrise*, the daily read, and swam off into a gorgeous kelp forest to find some peace and quiet.

LONG-LOST STEVE NOW JUST STEVE!
Steve, the son of rock stars Stevie and Steven, has been found! There's a party tonight at their mansion to celebrate his return. The dress code is FABULOUSLY FOUND: wear fabulous things you've found while being fabulous.
Every guest is asked to bring a smile and dye their hair their favourite colour of the rainbow!
We love you, Steve!

Steve rocked back and forth on a kelp strand like he was in a hammock.

'Who needs mermaids who leave you alone in leech spas when you can have rainbows and lots of seahorses with names really similar to yours in your life,' he said to himself.

Things were great.

Beattie had probably saved the world by now.

Even if she hadn't, someone else probably had.

A sparkly piece of kelp floated down to his eye level and began tap-dancing.

He smiled and carried on reading. But then something occurred to him. Slowly, he lowered the magazine.

'You're not … Razzle Dazzle kelp, are you?'

The sparkly kelp bowed and two other sparkly bits of kelp joined in the dancing.

Steve remembered the conversation they'd had with Maritza Mist about reversing magic. He could see Beattie, nodding sadly. And he could see Maritza explaining it all.

'*How can you tell if it's Razzle Dazzle kelp?*' came the voice from his memory in a long drawn-out groan.

'Because it's always showing off!' Steve cried, staring at the dancing kelp in awe. 'This is a MIRACLE! I'M A MIRACLE! Did you decide to come out of hiding for me because we're both miracles? I *AM* A MIRACLE! I can't wait to tell Zelda …'

34

To Mume

The mermaid Kingdom of Mume, hidden near the shores of Japan, was the most beautiful in the world.

Beattie and the others arrived at its centre, next to a peaceful garden of tiny coral clumps pruned to perfection. In the distance they could see bright lights and billboards.

'Look at the billboards,' Mimi said. 'It's Clippee!'

Clippee was Mimi's favourite cartoon character – a lobster in a dress, with an evil arch nemesis called O.

It made Beattie miss Steve even more – Clippee was his favourite too.

Mermaids with exquisitely painted tails glided past coral houses with seaweed walls. They smiled politely at the strange mermaids as they went by.

Beattie's hair turned blue.

'Your hair is doing that thing again,' Paris said, giving her a nudge.

Beattie pulled at her plait.

'No time to worry about your hair,' Zelda said. 'Meri, lead us to the ice creature!'

The Mume ice creature was in a vending machine, in the area of Mume known as Vending Machine City.

'You're joking,' Zelda said as they floated at the edge of a sprawling mass of machines. Things pinged and jingled, neon lights flashed and mermaids swam from place to place, putting money in slots and pulling strange items out.

'Here's one for merkitten accessories,' Beattie said.

Mimi fin-fued it slyly and a large shell fell out. Beattie cracked it open and found a tiny merkitten hat in the style of a narwhal.

'So this is the vending machine to use if you want to dress up your merkitten as a narwhal,' Zelda said. 'That's not weird.'

'IT'S BRILLIANT!' Paris said, swimming somersaults down the street over mermaids dressed in the

most fabulous costumes. Beattie swam past a mermaid wearing strings of glowing jellyfish-shaped earrings teamed with a glowing Clippee T-shirt.

'How are we ever going to find *the* vending machine?' Beattie despaired. 'There are thousands – maybe even millions of them.'

'Well, Vending Machine City is always growing,' Meri said. 'And every year they add more and more. The one Maritza hid the ice creature in is the first axolotl vending machine she ever created. But she made sure this one was broken – so no one could get the ice creature. It would sit among the millions of other vending machines, hidden forever.'

'It's actually quite a good hiding place,' Zelda said. 'And at least it's fun – Gulper and Rose are probably having to squeeze through a shark's bottom to get their ice creature.'

'Found it,' Mimi said casually.

Beattie raced over and inspected what Mimi was pointing at. It was an axolotl vending machine with a little *MM* scratched on the back. The sides were decorated

with pictures of mermaids with crazy curly hairstyles and sea-sprayed fringes holding up cute axolotls in tiny costumes – fish, turtle, shark, dolphin – you name it, the axolotls were wearing it. Behind the glass only the costumes remained; the axolotls were long gone.

'According to the list, the ice creature is a blobfish,' Meri said, trying to stick her head inside the flap at the bottom. 'It's probably hidden at the back, behind the costumes. Any idea how we get it out?'

Zelda swam up and plucked Grubs from Mimi's hand. 'Go get 'em, Grubs,' she said, feeding him into the flap.

They waited.

There was a rattling noise as Grubs disappeared through the costumes.

Beattie and Meri exchanged hopeful smiles. Mimi tapped her tail.

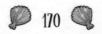

FOUR HOURS LATER

Zelda smooshed her face against the glass. 'He probably thinks we've put him away ...'

Meri fed Lady Wriggles into the flap to fetch him, and they waited again.

'Oh no,' she said, slapping a hand to her forehead. 'Lady Wriggles has one weakness—'

'She's a fragile jellyfish?' Zelda guessed.

'No,' Meri said. 'She's got a costume OBSESSION.'

They turned to see Lady Wriggles wriggling into a lobster costume.

'Mimi,' Beattie said. 'Fin-fu it open.'

Mimi flexed her tail and slapped it hard against the vending machine. It rolled over, but it didn't break.

'It's indestructible,' she said.

It was Paris's turn next. She shook her necklace and morphed into a shark.

Paris opened her jaws wide and charged, but her teeth barely made a dent.

'What did she make this out of?!' Meri cried, flicking it with her tail. 'Ow. Something solid.'

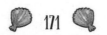 171

Beattie scrunched up her fist and closed her eyes.

'Oooh,' Zelda said, nudging Paris the shark. 'Beattie's going to do magic.'

Beattie knew she could make things happen if she tried really hard. She rolled up her tail and dug her nails into her palms. 'Come on, come on, come on,' she muttered.

There was a CLANG and a *crunch*. Something was happening!

Beattie opened her eyes and grinned – little axolotl costumes floated around her head. 'I did it!' she shouted. 'I broke the vending machine open!' She tried to raise her arms in triumph, but found she couldn't.

'Beattie!' Zelda cried. 'You're *in* the vending machine!'

35

Wearing a Vending Machine

Beattie moved at a sea-slug pace, the very tip of her tail poking out of the bottom of the vending machine. Grubs sat inside with her, on her head, and Lady Wriggles wrapped herself around her arm. Mermaids turned and stared as Beattie inched past them, making her way back to the portal. If they'd looked closely, they'd have seen she was clutching an ice blobfish in her hand.

'Almost there, Beatts,' Zelda said encouragingly as the others helped lift the vending machine from behind to stop it sinking.

'Are you holding the vending machine up to help me?' Beattie shouted, making bubbles form on the glass.

'No, no, you're doing it *all* yourself, you powerful water witch, you,' Meri lied, giving Zelda a wink.

They wriggled their way through the crowds of mermaids. Beattie watched as they pulled out seahorse-shaped hair accessories and cool T-shirts from various vending machines.

'Look,' Mimi said, hitting a machine with her tail as she passed. 'This one has Burguin T-shirts, and *Chops & Slinky*, the detective croc and eel duo cartoon from the Crocodile Kingdom. They have *everything*.'

'But *you* have the one thing *we* want,' came a familiar voice.

Beattie tried to spin round. 'Did I just hear—?'

'ROSE!' Rose screeched as her face popped up in front of the glass, making Beattie scream.

Zelda launched into attack mode, but Rose was too powerful. Her entire fist inflated and she knocked Zelda into a vending machine filled with dancing lobsters.

Meri was sent flying into an arguably better vending

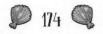

machine filled with delicious frozen Icetipple, and Paris the shark was slapped away as if she were a tiny fish.

Mimi held her finger up in a threatening fin-fu pose, but soon found herself tumbling on top of her twin.

'BYE-BYE,' said Gulper with a smirk as Rose advanced on Beattie.

'GIVE ME THE BLOBFISH!' she yelled.

Gulper held the vending machine still as Rose reached in and wrenched the ice blobfish from Beattie's grasp.

'DO SOMETHING, GRUBS!' Beattie cried, so Grubs had a nap.

Beattie tried to swim, but without the others holding up the vending machine she hit the seabed with a *clang*.

'Now all we have to do is get the Amberberg ice creature,' Rose said.

'WHAT?' Beattie said. 'But we came here because you were going to Amberberg!' She almost felt better – if they hadn't got the ice creature there, then they still had one more chance to stop them.

Rose and Gulper exchanged looks and sniggered. 'We just said that, you silly mermaid. We're immortal.

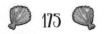

We have *forever* to find the ice creatures, so the only thing we have to do right now is stop you from getting any of them and slowing us down. You're not chasing us, Beattie Shelton. *We're* chasing *you.*'

Beattie stared wide-eyed as they disappeared into the distance.

The others came racing over, with various vending machine accessories in their hair. Meri crunched on an Icetipple icicle.

'It's over,' Beattie said from inside the vending machine.

Paris put both palms on the glass and fixed Beattie with a sincere stare. 'Come on, Beattie. It's not over until it's over.'

The vending machine made a whirring noise and a tiny dolphin outfit for an axolotl floated out.

They stared at it in silence.

'I suppose we might as well try,' Beattie finally said.

Paris was right. And she knew if Steve was still with them, he'd say the same thing.

Little did she know, Steve was headed her way.

 176

36

Back on the Dolphin Balloon

'BLEURGGGGHHH' went Steve as the dolphin balloon dived towards the water once more.

Only this time it was a swimming pool, because Steve had convinced the dolphin to take a shortcut across Australia.

'THERE'S SEAHORSE VOMIT IN THE SWIMMING POOL!' someone shouted as the dolphin flopped on, leaping from pool to pool.

'CRIPES!' Steve cried as they leapt off a cliff and hit the ocean, charging full pelt towards the icy waters of Frostopia.

'BE THERE SOON TO SAVE THE DAY, BEATTIE!' he called out as the Razzle Dazzle kelp jiggled about in the dolphin's mouth.

37

Goblin Sharks GALORE and an Unexpected Face

The whole city of Amberberg glowed in gorgeous hues of orange and gold. It was a mismatched place, filled with spectacular amber palaces and lumpy goblin sharks.

'It's this way,' Meri said. 'She hid the last ice creature – a starfish – in the old palace vaults.'

'*They're* in a rush,' Zelda said as they watched hundreds of mermaids trying to squeeze through the grand doors of the largest building in town – the old palace.

'I hear they have a star witness who can prove Gronnyupple stole the Amber Flubby,' a mermaid said to his friend as they swam past. 'I hope she goes to Viperview forever.'

'Gronnyupple!' Beattie said, spinning round, still in her vending machine.

Zelda turned to Meri and mouthed, 'Amber Flubby?'

'It's a jewel,' Meri said. 'The mermaids of Amberberg believe it's very powerful. It's not. But it is very expensive.'

'But what do we do?' Beattie asked. 'We can't have Gronnyupple sent to Viperview. And we can't let Gulper and Rose get the final ice creature.'

'We're in luck,' Meri said with a smile. 'Because Gronnyupple and the final ice creature are in the same building.'

Inside the old palace's courtroom, everyone was trying to swim closer to the front, hoping to get a look at the devious Gronnyupple in the flesh.

'She's a *criminal mastermind*,' one mermaid said.

'No she's not!' Zelda laughed.

Paris watched mermaids putting their handbags in the mouths of goblin sharks.

'What are they doing?'

'That's where they leave their bags. They collect them afterwards,' Meri explained.

'Mermaids are so weird,' Paris said.

'Humans are weirder,' Zelda said. 'I've seen a toaster.'

The crowd fell silent, apart from the mermaids next to Beattie's vending machine, who were giggling at her.

'It's fashion,' Beattie said. 'You'll all be wearing it soon.'

'Can I go now?' came a familiar voice from the front of the courtroom.

Zelda, Mimi and Paris craned their necks and spotted Gronnyupple. She looked smaller in the big watery room with the big important mermaids.

Zelda scrunched up her fists. 'We're about to see who framed Gronnyupple.'

'We call to the stand our STAR WITNESS, who saw Gronnyupple hide the Amber Flubby. This hero not only saw the criminal and reported her to us, but they also found the Amber Flubby and returned it to our city.' The judge mermaid held up a glob of amber.

The crowd went wild.

 181

'Silence, please. Allow our star witness to take the stand.'

A seahorse glided into the room.

Meri's mouth fell open.

Beattie and the others stared at her.

'What is it, Meri?' Zelda whispered.

'I know that seahorse,' Meri said in disbelief. 'It's Sabrina.'

38

Sabrina Explains Herself

The trial played out in slow motion for Meri as she tried to understand why Sabrina would have framed Gronnyupple.

'A seahorse runs Fortress Bay spy school,' Zelda said. It was the third time she'd said it, but she just couldn't quite get over it.

'Just my year,' Meri managed to say. She went to pull out her spy clamshell compact, but then realised she'd left it with Maritza to arrange Gronnyupple's rescue.

Meri gasped again.

'The shark,' she said. 'Remember when Maritza sent the Jawella's shark to save Gronnyupple and it failed? I thought someone had done some meddling magic, but I never considered the other way a mission could be stopped – and that's if someone at Fortress Bay called it

off at the last minute. The only one who has access to my clamshell compact and the authority to call things off is Sabrina.'

They all looked at the tiny seahorse.

'But why would she frame Gronnyupple?' Zelda said. 'And then stop her from being rescued?'

'Maybe she wanted to get her out of the way,' Meri said. 'Gronnyupple is a powerful water witch, after all.'

'But technically not as powerful as Beattie, who can *make* magic,' Zelda said. 'Why didn't they frame her too?'

'If there's no good reason why Sabrina would frame Gronnyupple, we must be missing something,' Beattie said.

'MERI!' came a tiny seahorse shout. 'What are you doing in Amberberg?'

Meri tried to hide under the crowds, but it was no good – they parted, revealing her lying face down in the sand.

She looked up at Sabrina.

'Oh … hi,' she said sheepishly.

'Meri,' Sabrina hissed. 'Get out of here now – and take your friends and the … vending machine … with you.'

Beattie growled at Sabrina.

'Get them out of here. I've got this under control,' Sabrina snapped.

'Oh I bet you do, traitor!' Meri cried. 'You framed Gronnyupple, and she's my friends' friend.'

'You're a spy, Meri,' Sabrina whispered. 'You can't have friends.'

'I'm her friend,' Mimi said, putting her arm around Meri.

Zelda slunk off undetected to the vaults to get the ice creature.

Beattie swivelled in her vending machine and spotted two mermaids in large amber hats heading that way too.

'IT'S GULPER AND ROSE!' Beattie cried, trying to point but hitting the vending machine glass instead. 'IN BIG AMBER HATS!'

Paris looked around. Almost everyone was wearing big amber hats.

 185

'They're closing in on Zelda,' Beattie said. 'Paris, go! Get the ice creature and stop them.'

Paris nodded and patted the vending machine, making more axolotl costumes fall out.

'I'm on it!'

She shook the necklace and morphed into a jellyfish. Beattie watched helplessly from her vending machine as her friend wafted through the crowds.

'GRONNYUPPLE WONDRA CRAB,' the judge said.

'OH LOOK!' Gronnyupple cheered, spotting Paris the jellyfish. 'It's my friend Paris!'

'That's a jellyfish,' the judge said flatly. 'And I'm afraid, Gronnyupple, we have decided you are GUILTY.'

'What?!' Beattie shouted.

Sabrina shot off.

'GET HER!' Beattie yelled. Mimi and Meri lifted Beattie and wobbled outside – and suddenly saw a familiar restaurant.

'The Jawella's shark,' Mimi said, bowing grandly. 'Good day, sir.'

Sabrina stared at Mimi.

'She's the weird one,' Meri whispered. 'Incredible fin-fu skills though.'

The thick amber door behind them flew open, revealing Gronnyupple.

'Beattie!' Gronnyupple cheered, staring at the vending machine. 'You've got a new look! It's very … rectangular!'

The Jawella's shark opened its mouth wide.

Gronnyupple looked at Beattie and Mimi and then Meri.

'Oh hello,' she said. 'You're a new one!'

Sabrina began to guide Gronnyupple into the shark.

'YOU CAN'T DO THIS!' Meri cried. 'SHE'S MY FRIENDS' FRIEND!'

'Meri,' Sabrina hissed. 'This isn't real – it's a set-up. It was all planned. I've been trying to get hold of a water witch to help out with lessons at the spy school, but they're so difficult to find. So I framed this one for a fake crime, and now I'm going to tell her she can either go to Viperview or teach a few classes.'

'That's so sneaky,' Meri said.

Sabrina shrugged. 'I never said I was nice. This is how spies work.'

'You could've just asked her,' Meri said. 'Gronnyupple is really kind, and if you got to know her, she'd definitely help you.'

'No time for that emotional stuff,' Sabrina scoffed. 'This was more effective.'

'Oooh,' Gronnyupple said from inside Jawella's. 'It's a restaurant in here!'

The shark took off, soaring high over the Amberberg buildings.

'Meri, some things are beyond your spy grade,' Sabrina said. 'You need to stop meddling. It's time to come back to spy school with me.'

'But we're not finished yet,' Beattie said, as Mimi took Meri's hand and held it tightly.

'We still have to stop Gulper and Rose,' Mimi said. 'And Meri is helping us.'

Sabrina rolled her eyes. 'They. Are. In. Viperview. Locked away! Meri, stop spreading such nonsense!'

'But Gulper and Rose never went back to Viperview!' Meri cried. 'They used a doubling potion to double themselves – that's why Gulper said "FISH EYE!" It's a side effect of the potion!'

'It's true,' Beattie said. 'I've used that potion myself.'

'Gulper and Rose are collecting ice creatures,' Meri blurted out, scared to say the next bit. 'And they have the ice narwhal, Sabrina. I was late checking it one day, and when I got there, Gulper and Rose had stolen it. I lost the ice narwhal.'

Meri's tail suddenly felt lighter – it was such a relief to admit her big mistake. She wished she'd done it sooner, maybe then things wouldn't be so bad now.

'But I saw the ice narwhal after you left. It was there, safe in the lock-up,' Sabrina said.

Meri shifted awkwardly.

'I made Lady Wriggles make a fake one. She was just being loyal to me.'

Sabrina floated on the spot, her mouth hanging open. 'Well, this is a disaster.'

'It's all under control,' Beattie said. 'We have a plan.'

 189

'I don't know how to say this without sounding mean,' Sabrina said, 'but you're telling me everything is under control while trapped inside a vending machine.'

'I GOT IT!' Zelda roared, swimming straight into the vending machine and knocking herself out. A tiny ice starfish floated down and landed on the bit of Beattie's tail hanging out of the machine.

'WE DID IT!' Beattie cheered, but Gulper and Rose weren't finished with them yet.

THE FREEZY

Frostopia's Coolest Magazine!

BURGUIN INTERVIEW!

Today we interviewed Kiko Frostwater of Slushville, who has found the rare and elusive Upside-Down Burguin! Upside-Down Burguin looks like Original Burguin, but due to a factory malfunction, his head is sticking out of the bottom of the burger bun and his flippers are sticking out of the top.

Reporter: Kiko, you found Upside-Down Burguin — what is the first thing you did when you realised it was a special collector's item?

Kiko: Took it apart and stuck it back together the right way.

Reporter: So ... now it's not the rare and special Upside-Down Burguin, it's just an Original Burguin?

Kiko: I think so!

Reporter: But you can get Original Burguins every-where, there was only one Upside-Down Burguin in the whole world!

Kiko: And I fixed him.

Reporter: Thank you, Kiko …

39

Showdown

Sabrina screamed as Gulper and Rose tried to grab the ice starfish.

'STOP THAT!' Beattie cried, curling her tail around the tiny creature.

Rose rolled her eyes and flung the vending machine up high, where it smashed into the amber spires, splitting in two.

'I'M FREE!' Beattie bellowed as she tumbled out with Grubs and Lady Wriggles.

She tore the ice creature from Rose's grasp and chucked it at Zelda, who caught it and dived through the portal to Realm Reach.

Everyone followed, fighting to squeeze through the portal first.

'Sorry I doubted you!' Sabrina called faintly to Meri.

 193

Meri smiled and dived into the portal.

'You look weird without the vending machine,' Mimi said to Beattie as they also tumbled back through to icy waters. 'I'd got used to you wearing it.'

'GIVE US THE ICE CREATURE!' Gulper yelled.

Zelda threw it to Paris.

'NEVER!' Paris cried, as it began to crack in her hand.

'Keep hold of it!' Beattie shouted. 'Don't let go!'

Rose growled and hurtled towards Paris, who held the ice starfish behind her back. But Rose wasn't after the ice creature. Before anyone could stop her, she ripped the necklace from Paris's neck and smashed it against the ice. She cackled madly as what remained of it sank to the bottom of the sea.

'NO!' Beattie screamed. 'She's morphing back into a human!'

Paris's tail stretched and began forming into legs and feet. She puffed out her cheeks and looked up in panic – there was nothing but solid ice above her.

'DON'T WORRY, A MIRACLE IS COMING!' came a familiar voice as a seahorse whizzed past Beattie's nose and halted in front of Paris.

'Steve's back?' Beattie said in astonishment.

Paris smiled, her face pale and her eyes slowly beginning to close.

'I'LL SAVE HER!' Steve shouted, blowing urgently into her ear.

'That's not her *mouth*, Steve,' Zelda said, hurrying over.

'Oh,' Steve said. 'Is that not how you do it?'

Beattie grabbed the necklace from the seabed. She could feel her tail getting hot. Her hair began to change colour, from blue to pink to green to orange to black to red. She summoned her powers, holding the necklace up as high as she could, thinking only of Paris. She couldn't stop her hands from shaking.

'How's it going, dears?' Maritza Mist said as she arrived on the scene. 'Oh, not well.'

The tiny sea creatures that had fallen off the necklace reappeared around Beattie's colour-changing hair.

'Wow,' Maritza whispered to no one. 'She's good.'

Beattie held on tightly to the necklace and focused all her energy. Her tail felt like it was on fire. Her fingers tingled as if there was magic trapped inside them.

'I'LL FIX IT!' she screamed as the necklace re-formed itself. She flopped over, exhausted.

'Paris!' Meri cried, grabbing the necklace and securing it around her neck.

She held Paris's unmoving body in her arms.

'Paris?' she whispered.

'NOOOOO!' Steve wailed. 'NOT PARIS!'

But then Paris's feet began to wriggle.

The knee-high socks she was wearing started to unravel.

'IT'S WORKING!' Meri cried. 'BEATTIE, YOU DID IT!'

Paris's eyes snapped open and she took a deep watery breath. She was a mermaid again!

'Nice tail,' Rose said mockingly. 'But I have something nicer. I have the ice starfish, and that makes ALL OF THEM.'

She started placing them on her tail, one by one. With each ice creature she added, she grew frostier and frostier.

'It would be funny if she turned into one of those human snowmen, wouldn't it?' Zelda joked.

Beattie shot her a look.

'OK. Not the right time for snowman jokes,' Zelda said.

'We always knew we'd get out of Viperview and finish what we started,' Rose boasted to Maritza. 'Did you think you could stop us with some amateur water witches and *normal* mermaids?'

Paris charged at Rose, but she batted her away like she was a shrimp.

Beattie tried too, but found herself crumpled in a heap next to Paris.

'HELLO THERE!' Gronnyupple's voice called over the confusion. Up above, a shark circled. 'I got the Jawella's shark to drop me off here! I'm going to teach a class at Fortress Bay Spy Sch—'

She stopped when she saw Gulper and Rose.

'*She skates, she slides*,' came a voice from nearby.

Gronnyupple grinned as the Blubble seal swam past. 'I found the seal! What a day!'

'Come *here*,' Zelda hissed at Gronnyupple.

Together, Beattie, Mimi, Zelda, Maritza Mist, Paris, Meri and Gronnyupple lined up to face Rose.

'Now what?' Meri asked.

'We start a band?' Zelda joked.

Steve interrupted, the stream of Razzle Dazzle kelp curled around his tail. 'Beattie, I have so many questions about what your hair is doing, but no time right now. I found this – it's the Razzle Dazzle kelp Maritza said can reverse spells. You know, make Gulper and Rose *not* immortal any more.'

'Are you sure it's Razzle Dazzle kelp?' Beattie whispered excitedly.

Rose laughed. 'WE'RE GOING TO RULE THE WORLD!' She fixed her eyes on Beattie. 'And no magic mermaid will survive. Well, we'll keep Maritza as a servant, so she can make potions for us. But we'll get rid of the rest.'

Maritza sighed. 'I never should have made that immortality paste.'

Rose's face was frosty now, and she had only a few ice creatures left to add before her tail was complete. 'I'LL PROBABLY MAKE THEM STAMP PICTURES OF MY FACE ON ALL CLAM CARS TOO. OR MAYBE I'LL CRUSH ALL THE CLAM CARS WITH MY ALL-POWERFUL FISTS!'

Maritza spotted the Razzle Dazzle kelp and her eyes lit up. 'Gulper and Rose need to hold it,' she mouthed. 'And then they need to say the magic word – *cigamdiamrem*.'

'What?!' Beattie mouthed back.

'It's "mermaid magic" backwards,' Maritza whispered.

She watched as Rose continued to attach the ice creatures to her tail. The others looked to Beattie for directions, but Beattie didn't know what to do.

'I'm willing to sing,' Steve whispered. 'Would opera be helpful?'

'Leave this to me,' Zelda said, pulling at her waistcoat. 'Hey, Rose!'

'Yes, Zelda,' Rose said with a sigh.

'Can you remind me what happens when you've added all those little ice creatures to your tail?'

'THEN I BECOME ALL-POWERFUL AND THE MERMAID WORLD IS MINE!'

'So what about you?' Zelda said to Gulper. 'You get nothing? You did half the work!'

Gulper looked down at the ice creatures he was handing Rose. 'Wait, why don't I get to be all-powerful?'

'*Because*,' Rose spat, 'only one mermaid can wear all the ice creatures. So only *I* can become all powerful. You get to hang out with me, that's all you get.'

'But *I* could wear all the ice creatures,' Gulper said.

Rose laughed. 'Don't be RIDICULOUS!'

Zelda flashed Beattie a smug smile.

'What's so ridiculous about it?' Gulper said, his voice sharp.

'Oh come on, Gulper,' Rose said. 'It's *you*.'

'She may not be magic,' Mimi said, 'but my twin is *excellent* at causing trouble.'

Beattie's hair turned pink.

'Your hair is doing that thing again,' Mimi said.

'Now what?' Meri asked.

'I WOULD BE SO MUCH BETTER AT RULING THE WORLD!' Gulper roared at Rose.

'NO YOU WOULDN'T!' Rose scoffed. 'AND ANYWAY, MY FACE WILL LOOK SO MUCH BETTER ON ALL THE SEAWEED FLAGS I'M GOING TO MAKE – FOR EVERY MERMAID CITY IN THE WORLD!'

'WELL AT LEAST THAT'LL BE *TERRIFYING*!' Gulper said.

'YEAH!' Rose cheered before stopping. 'Wait,' she said. 'DID YOU JUST MAKE FUN OF MY FACE?'

'At least they don't have that new magical kelp that would allow them *both* to become all-powerful,' Beattie said loudly.

Gulper swam fast towards her and snatched it.

'Oh no,' Beattie said, winking excitedly at Zelda. 'What a disaster.'

'Aha!' Gulper said, swimming eagerly over to Rose. 'This will split the magic.'

'But I don't want to split the magic!' Rose said, grabbing the other end of the kelp.

They pulled and pulled until it snapped in two.

'It smells weird, what did you say it was?' Rose asked, sniffing it.

'Cigamdiamrem,' Beattie said with a smile.

'Cigamdiamrem?' Gulper and Rose both said at once.

'Is that even a word?' Rose said as she tried to throw it away. But she couldn't – it was stuck to her fingers.

'NO!' Gulper cried, realising his mistake. He shook his hand furiously, but the kelp wouldn't budge.

In a snap, the pair grew older and older, morphing and twisting until they disappeared with a *pop*.

'IT WORKED!' Beattie cried.

Paris picked up the ice narwhal and held it firmly in her hands. It began to crack.

'Come on,' Beattie whispered, willing it to work.

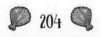

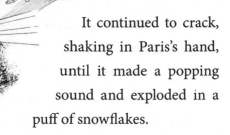

It continued to crack, shaking in Paris's hand, until it made a popping sound and exploded in a puff of snowflakes.

They all watched as the sparkle of magic within the other ice creatures faded. The magic was finally broken.

'NO WAY! WE DID IT!' Beattie roared as Meri, Zelda, Mimi and Gronnyupple swam in victory circles around Paris, cheering and slapping their tails together.

Steve and Sabrina eyed each other suspiciously.

'Are you Long-lost Steve?' she asked.

'Sort of,' Steve said.

'I'm your sister,' Sabrina said. 'But I'm a really important spy, so I won't be home much.'

'Steve!' Beattie said, grinning madly. 'You still have a little bit of Razzle Dazzle kelp stuck in your tail.' She held it up.

There was a cough. She looked over to see Maritza floating quietly.

'I was wondering,' Maritza Mist said, eyeing the kelp in Beattie's hand, 'if we could do one final reverse spell.'

Beattie smiled. 'Sure! On what?'

'On me, dear,' Maritza said. 'It's time for me to go.'

40

Goodbye, Maritza Mist

Beattie's face fell. 'You want to be gone forever?'

The seal in the Blubble costume floated behind Beattie, playing the jingle,

She skates, she glides, she moves from side to side.
She's big and she's trouble,
Yeah ... she's Blubble.

'Unbelievable,' Beattie muttered as the seal disappeared into the Mume portal.

'I've been here too long,' Maritza said. 'No one wants to live forever.'

'But you're SEVEN,' Zelda said.

Maritza Mist laughed. 'I only *look* seven. I'm actually four thousand and eight years old. And four

days, if you're counting, which I have been, believe me.'

'Aw no,' Mimi said. 'We just missed your birthday!'

'You can free me, Beattie, after all these years!' Maritza said.

'But I don't want you to go,' Beattie said sadly. 'We've only just got to know you. And who is going to send out your magic catalogue orders?'

'Why, Gronnyupple, of course!'

'Seriously?' Zelda whispered. 'Have you seen her use magic?!'

Maritza Mist smiled. 'There's no one who loves magic more than Gronnyupple, plus she wouldn't be alone. She'd have Beattie to make the magic for her.'

'Me?' Beattie spluttered.

'Dear, you are much better at making magic than I ever was. And look, your hair is changing with your moods, like the true chosen one.'

'I thought she might have a disease,' Mimi confided to Maritza.

 208

'That always happens when you start making magic,' Maritza said. 'It calms down after a while.'

'Wait,' Zelda said. 'Beattie's hair has gone a deep blue. What does that mean?'

'Sad,' Beattie said as a tear rolled down her face. She took the last remaining bit of kelp and held it in her hand.

Gronnyupple hugged Maritza Mist tightly. 'Thank you for the wonderful water-witch potions, and for always delivering my catalogue orders on time, apart from that last one.'

Maritza beamed at her. 'And thank you for being my favourite customer, and for knowing there was trouble ahead and acting so quickly. Your instincts are good, Gronnyupple. Look after Grubs for me.'

Steve, Mimi, Zelda and Paris took it in turns to hug Maritza goodbye.

'And goodbye, Beattie,' she said. 'Don't be doing any more spells near vending machines.'

'It really has been one of the greatest things in my life to have met you,' Beattie said, slowly handing Maritza Mist the kelp.

Maritza took the kelp and held it tightly. 'Goodbye, dears.'

Beattie closed her eyes as Maritza whispered the magic word.

It all happened so fast. First, Maritza morphed into a teenager!

'Ooooh!' Steve said.

Then a mermaid in her thirties.

'Aaaaah!' Steve said.

Then a mermaid in her sixties, then eighties, then nineties.

'Yeulch,' Steve said.

'Oh stop being such an ageist little seahorse,' Zelda said.

Old Maritza Mist smiled and waved one final time.

And then she was gone.

41

Back to Underwater Igloo Avenue

The mermaids floated sadly back to Maritza Mist's house.

'I think I'll come here and run the catalogue from Maritza's house when I'm not visiting Fortress Bay,' Gronnyupple said. 'I'm a big fan of the frost. And the fashion. And as long as Realm Reach is there, I can easily get back to the Crocodile Kingdom to stock up on Seahorse Surprise! Hey, Beattie,' she rambled on excitedly. 'Maybe you could create a potion that makes Seahorse Surprise.'

'Mmm, maybe,' Beattie said as she swam on ahead, though she wasn't really listening.

'Oh, Beattie,' Steve said, opening up the false teeth. 'Thank you for getting me this wonderful rainbow-coloured pillow!'

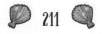

Beattie peered in to see the rainbowfish lying flat in the false teeth.

'That's not a pillow,' Zelda said, relishing the opportunity to annoy him. 'That's your new ROOMMATE.'

42

Just Mermaids

Beattie, Mimi and Zelda were back in the twins' bedroom in Periwinkle Palace in the Hidden Lagoon. Zelda was practising her shockey moves and Mimi was slumped on the bed with a foam shake as she caught up on all the episodes of *Clippee* that she'd missed.

Beattie rested her elbows on the window ledge and looked out on the Swirlyshell streets below. Mermaids with all kinds of tails floated past: black and white whale ones from Frostopia, crocodile prints from the Crocodile Kingdom, Mume tails and Jewelport and Beluga Town! ones.

The whole mermaid world was talking about Beattie and her friends who had taken on Gulper and Rose and won. News about Realm Reach had spread, and now

the realms were united once more. Mermaids could travel the world, seeing the sights and making new friends.

'No point in being ice-olated,' Zelda had joked.

The little clamshell compact on the twins' desk began buzzing. Zelda picked it up and threw it across the room. 'Beatts, it's for you!'

There on the shell screen was Gronnyupple's face. Grubs was asleep on her head, snoring loudly.

'How are the new spells coming along, Beattie? I'm getting ready to send the next catalogue out.'

'Almost there!' Beattie said. 'It's going to be the best one yet.'

'Have you made the spell that makes you melt?'

Beattie shook her head. 'Too dangerous.'

'I wouldn't like to be slushy forever, that's true,' Gronnyupple said.

The clamshell compact began buzzing again. 'Oh, I've got another call.'

Paris appeared on the screen next to Gronnyupple.

'It's Paris!' Beattie called over to Zelda and Mimi.

'How is it being a human again?' Zelda asked.

Paris rolled her eyes. 'It's hideous! I have so many toes! AND KNEES!'

They all burst out laughing.

The clam compact jiggled and Meri popped up on the screen too.

'I have five minutes between spy classes,' she said as Lady Wriggles floated past in the background. 'Sabrina said my method of spying is so good I'm going to be given my first official mission!'

'Cool!' Zelda said.

'We miss you!' Beattie added.

'I'm going to come and see you soon, if I can sneak away,' Paris said. 'Is everything going well with the catalogue?'

'Oh yes!' Gronnyupple said. 'Tell her about your new thing, Beattie. The special one.'

Beattie held up some rings with different-shaped gems – a dolphin, a shell, a pufferfish … 'Well, I took the magic that makes my hair change colour and I put it into these rings. I call them *mood rings*. When

you wear them, they'll show your mood in a colour.'

'ISN'T IT AMAZING?!' Gronnyupple roared, spitting Seahorse Surprise all over the screen.

Zelda put hers on and it flashed all the colours of the rainbow. Mimi's did too.

'What does that mean?' Zelda asked.

'Happy,' Beattie said with a smile.

Steve sailed in through the window, carrying a multicoloured seahorse mansion. Zelda's ring instantly flicked to yellow.

'What's yellow?' Gronnyupple shouted through the screen.

'Annoyed,' Beattie whispered.

'Oh, thank you *so much*, Mimi, for saying we could keep our mansion here until we find a permanent location,' Steve said, dumping it on top of Zelda's shockey gear.

Zelda growled.

Stevie and Steven, Steve's parents, came swishing through the window, blowing into shells and making an irritating honking noise.

 217

Zelda covered her ears.

'They're rock stars,' Steve said proudly.

'So you're moving here for good?' Mimi asked Stevie and Steven.

'For half the year,' Steven said. 'We'll do six months in Rainbow Landing and the other half here – bringing our mansion with us!'

Another little seahorse swam into the room. 'And this,' Steve said, 'is my big sister, Sabrina.'

'Hi, Sabrina,' everyone chimed.

They knew exactly who Sabrina was, but they couldn't let Steve's parents know, because of the top-secret spy thing.

'You really should visit Rainbow Landing,' Stevie said, rubbing her nose against Mimi's. 'They'd love your rainbow tail!'

Beattie's mum, the travel writer Belinda Shelton, sailed past the window with her notepad. 'Mimi, are you ready?'

'Oh yes,' Mimi said, switching off the *Clippee* cartoon and swimming out of the window.

'We're off to Hammerhead Heights to interview the Jawella's shark for *Clamzine*. Mimi is going to translate for me.'

'Ugh, I wish I was there!' Paris cried from the clamshell compact.

'Where are you right now, Paris? We could pick you up!' Beattie's mum offered. 'It's so easy now with Realm Reach!'

Beattie snapped the compact closed. 'She's really far away.'

'Let's all meet at Jawella's for dinner tonight then!' Beattie's mum called back.

Beattie opened the clamshell compact to a smiling Paris, Gronnyupple and Meri.

'Why don't you tell your mum that Paris is a human on land?' Gronnyupple whispered. 'Your mum is cool, and she's not anti-human.'

'Because I don't want to listen to all the questions she'll have about toes!' Beattie said. 'I'll send you each a mood ring. Look out for a crabagram!'

And with that they said goodbye.

Zelda flopped on to her bed. 'Beattie, given everything we've achieved, I think it's officially official.'

'What is?' Beattie said.

Zelda grinned. 'We are *bad*.'

There is a world where
witches live, deep down
below the sink pipes ...

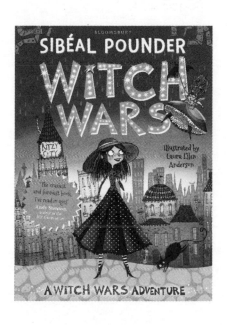

Read on for a sneak peek at the
first book in Sibéal Pounder's
Witch Wars series

AVAILABLE NOW!

Down the Plughole

It would have been very difficult to spot Fran the fairy on the day this story begins. Her dress may have been puffy, her hair may have been huge, but she was barely the size of a small potato.

Fran was slowly sidestepping across a garden lawn, holding a large, limp leaf in front of her. She didn't want the owner of the garden to see her because Miss Heks was a terrible old woman with a grim face and size eleven shoes. If she had seen Fran she would've squashed her immediately.

Fran and her leaf were on a mission. There was something very important in the shed at the bottom of Miss Heks's garden. That something was a girl called Tiga Whicabim.

'You!' Tiga said, pointing at a slug that was sliding its way across an old stone sink. 'You will be the star of my show! You will play the role of Beryl, an ambitious dancer with severe hiccups.'

Tiga had been in the shed for hours. The evil Miss Heks had been her guardian for as long as Tiga could remember and she had quickly learned to keep out of her way. If she didn't, the old bat would make her sew up the holes in her disgusting, scratchy dresses. Or she would force Tiga to run up and down the garden in her gigantic, ugly shoes, bellowing things like 'FASTER!' and 'OH, DID YOU TRIP?' from the kitchen window.

Tiga shone a torch on the slug.

'You are going to be the best actor the world has ever seen!' she cried.

Fran sighed when she saw that.

Not because she'd finally found Tiga, after a long and perilous journey that had almost ended with her being eaten by a dog.

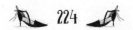

No, the reason Fran sighed was because she loved a bit of acting!

Despite her small size, Fran was a big deal in the world of show business. Everyone called her Fran the Fabulous Fairy (a name she had made up for herself). She had hosted many award-winning TV shows like *Cooking for Tiny People* and *The Squashed and the Swatted* and she'd played the lead role in *Glittery Sue* – a tragic drama about a small lady called Sue who got some glitter in her hair and couldn't get it out again.

'An actor you say!' Fran said, making Tiga jump.

Tiga stared, mouth open, at the small person that marched across the shed and – very ungracefully, and with much grunting – climbed up the leg of her trusty old rocking chair.

Fran stretched out a hand.

'Very delighted to meet you, Tiga! Now, it's pronounced *Teega*, isn't it? That's what I thought! I'm very good at names and absolutely everything else. I'm Fran the Fabulous Fairy. But you can call me Fran. Or Fabulous. BUT NEVER JUST FAIRY. I hate that.'

Tiga, understandably, assumed she had gone mad. Or at the very least fallen asleep.

She squinted at the little thing with big hair and then looked to the slug for reassurance, but it was sliding its way across the floor as if it knew exactly who Fran was, and was trying to escape.

'I don't think,' Fran said, pointing at the slug, 'that she should be acting in the lead role. She is slimy and not paying much attention.'

Fran wiggled a foot and a beehive of hair just like her own appeared on top of the slug's head.

'Much, much, *much* better,' she said.

Tiga panicked – the slug had *hair*! Not any old hair, a beehive of perfectly groomed hair! It was a split-second reaction, but with a flick of her hand she batted the fairy clean off the rocking chair.

Fran wobbled from left to right and tried to steady herself.

'Did you just *swat* me?' she snapped. 'The ultimate insult!'

Tiga tried to avoid eye contact and instead looked at

the slug. She couldn't be sure, but it looked a lot like it was shaking its head at her.

'WITCHES ARE NOT ALLOWED TO SWAT FAIRIES. IT IS THE LAW,' Fran ranted.

'I'm sorry!' Tiga cried. 'I didn't think you were real – I thought you were just my imagination! You don't need to call me a witch.'

'Yes I do,' said Fran, floating in front of Tiga with her hands on her hips. 'Because you are one.'

'I am one what?' Tiga asked.

'One witch,' said Fran as she twirled in the air, got her puffy dress caught in her wings and crash-landed on the floor.

'BRAAAAT!' came a bellow from across the garden. 'Time to leave the shed. Your dinner is ready!'

Tiga glanced nervously out of the window. 'If you are real, although I'm still not convinced you are, you'd better leave now. Miss Heks is a terrible old woman and she will do horrible, nasty, ear-pinching things to you.'

Fran ignored her and went back to twirling in the air. 'What are you having for dinner?'

'Cheese water,' Tiga said with a sigh. 'It's only ever cheese water.'

Fran thought about this for a moment. 'And how do you make this cheese water?'

'You find a bit of mouldy old cheese and you put it in some boiling water,' said Tiga, looking ill.

Fran swooped down lower and landed on the sink. 'Well, I'm afraid we don't have cheese water in Ritzy City – it's mostly cakes.'

Tiga stared at the fairy. 'Ritzy where?'

'*Riiiitzzzzzy Ciiiiity!*' Fran cheered, waving her hands in the air.

Tiga shrugged. 'Never heard of it.'

'But you're a witch,' said Fran.

'I am not a witch!' Tiga cried.

'You SO are!'

'I am not!'

'Definitely are,' said Fran, nodding her head. 'Even your name says so.'

And with that she flicked her tiny finger, sending a burst of glittery dust sailing across the room.

TIGA WHICABIM, the dust read.

Then it began to wobble and rearrange itself into something new.

I AM A BIG WITCH.

'You've cheated somehow,' Tiga mumbled, moving the dust letters about in the air. Most people would've believed Fran by this point, but Tiga wasn't used to magic and fun and insane fairies. So, despite this very

convincing evidence that she might just be a witch, Tiga still walked towards the door. Towards the cheese water.

'TIGA!' bellowed Miss Heks. 'YOUR CHEESE WATER HAS REACHED BOILING POINT.'

'Cheese water,' Fran chuckled. 'Wait! Where are you going, Tiga?'

'To eat dinner,' said Tiga. 'Bye, Fabulous Fairy Fran. It was lovely to meet you.'

Fran raised a hand in the air. 'Wait! *What?* You're not coming with me to Ritzy City, a place of wonder and absolutely no cheese?'

Tiga paused. Even if it was a mad dream, it was better than cheese water. She turned on her heel and walked back towards Fran.

Fran squealed and squeaked and did somersaults in the air.

'WHAT'S GOING ON IN THERE? I KNOW YOU CAN HEAR ME, YOU LITTLE MAGGOT!' Miss Heks shouted.

Tiga could see Miss Heks stomping her way towards the shed.

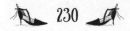

'Quick!' Fran cried. 'We must go to Ritzy City right now!'

'*How?*' Tiga cried, frantically looking around the shed for an escape route.

'Down the sink pipes, of course,' Fran said as she shot through the air and straight down the plughole.

'Come on, Tiga!' her shrill little voice echoed from somewhere inside the sink.

Tiga leaned over the stone sink and stared down the plughole.

There was nothing down there. No light. And certainly no city, that was for sure.

The door to the shed flew open and splinters of old wood went soaring through the air.

'WHAT IS GOING ON?' Miss Heks bellowed.

'NOW!' Fran yelled.

Tiga wiggled a finger in the plughole.

This is nonsense, she thought, just as she disappeared.

Find out where it all began

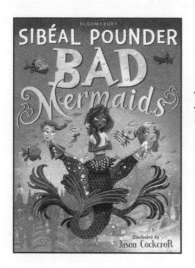